I0594312

Gellibrand and Hesse

Gellibrand and Hesse

Brett G Hogan

Copyright © 2019 Brett G Hogan
All rights reserved.
ISBN-13: 978-0-6489340-0-4

This second edition published by Brett G Hogan in
Melbourne, Australia.
September 2020

Cover image: Photo courtesy of pexels.com
Additional cover artwork by Indigenous artist
Georgia Hogan

Table of Contents

Chapter one 1
Chapter two 18
Chapter three 43
Chapter four 45
Chapter five 47
Chapter six 69
Chapter seven 93
Chapter eight 99
Chapter nine 127
Chapter ten 155
Chapter eleven 163
Chapter twelve 191
Bibliography 208

Chapter one

Although it was spring, it was not cold as the sun climbed higher over the starboard bow. It had been a harrowing and icy trip from Hobart, but that made the entrance through the heads into the sunny bay seem all the more pleasant, in comparison to that experience. The seas around the south of Van Diemen's Land boiled and agitated. The large swell seemed to emanate from a source deep below the surface, so that even in calm weather the seas rocked and swelled as though from some innate power that arose from the depths of that cold dark water.

He preferred to lay down on the deck and gaze upward at the sky when sailing under these now pristine conditions than look about at the land. So that he could forget about the drama of sailing in rough seas and relax and feel the way the ship rode with the sea and the wind, rather than in a battle against the elements. At times like these he almost enjoyed travelling by sea. When he gazed at the sky through the rigging he felt at ease with the movements of the ship, as the movement of the ship in turn felt at ease with the sea.

The crew was not so much at ease though, as the wind that brought the warmth to the air from the north-west, also required them to tack frequently to work up the narrow straight and into the open expanse of the bay proper. Jagged rocks on each side of the heads were clear warning to stay within the channel now referred to as just 'the rip'. This straight through the entrance was barley more than half a mile wide and was known to have claimed several ships in the short time since it had been discovered for use as a shipping port.

Mr. Taylor though, lay very much oblivious to this labouring of the crew, as he observed through the rigging the gulls drifting on the wind and the few high clouds whispering on the upper winds. The sheets creaked and strained as the ship gently rolled with the gusts of breeze pressing the vessel ever forward. His job would begin when the ship anchored and the cargo put ashore. He knew there were tireless weeks ahead in new and dangerous lands. He savoured this opportunity to rest while he gathered his thoughts and to preserve his strength.

The cargo was not so pleased with the warm weather which was evidenced by the increasing and constant bleating that came from below. The 800-odd head of sheep cramped into the hold were stirring as though they could sense that land was again close by. It would be at least a few hours more that they would have to endure the cramped and humid atmosphere of the leaky timber hull. The heat would take a toll on the stressed animals and Taylor was aware that time could not be spared if the valuable livestock were to reach the shore in full numbers.

Frederick Taylor and his mate Harry Sutherland had been charged with getting this herd of prime breeding stock from Van Diemen's Land to an area of the mainland ripe for the picking by entrepreneurial investors and farmers now scrambling to take up the best sheep runs. While the areas around Sydney and Hobart had established farming lands that were quickly spreading to take up the demand for produce by the growing local population, each of those towns had the restriction of bush and mountains very close by, that hampered the ease at which new lands could be cleared and developed for farming.

The mainland however, to the north of the island of Van Diemen's Land, and three hundred and fifty miles south-west of Sydney, had many hundreds of square miles of virgin fertile plains. These plains were interspersed with clean freshwater streams and covered by native grasses that could water and feed many thousands of sheep. Not to mention the extent of production once water troughs and European pasture grasses could be introduced to improve the grazing potential exponentially.

As the sun climbed toward midday Taylor approached the captain of the ship, an old crusty Irishman, as Sutherland peered on anxiously. "I didn't know it was going to take so long to get from the open sea to the landing area Captain. If those sheep are not freed from the hull of the ship soon, by the sound of them, they might start dying".

"Well I didn't know it was going to be so fucking hot, Mr Taylor. And in the springtime! Why anyone would want to come to this desolate dusty shithole is beyond me. But anyhow, the northerly wind has been against us, but at least we have *some* wind to work with. The ship will be at the beach just around the head you can see over there soon enough and you can get the sheep ashore then." The captain paused for a while looking sideways at Taylor he added in a curious tone "Why didn't your boss just get this lot unloaded at the Yarra river along with everything else? At least they have a makeshift port built there where it is deep enough for a ship this size to dock".

"You know why" Taylor replied, "This lot don't belong to the Association. These sheep are going to the land west of the river that is the boundary of the land the Association claim to have bought from the blacks. You see that short row of mountains sticking out at the north end of the bay?" The Captain nodded as his gaze swept the horizon where a geographic formation known as the You Yangs was clearly defined against the blue sky, maybe thirty or forty miles away. "We are taking this mob to the land straight past those mountains to take up a run on the plains. It will be the best run west of the Yarra Yarra region. Just over the next river from the association land, where the town and port will continue to grow. But this is on land that is not owned by anyone, and out of the control of those snooty Association bastards."

The Captain grunted and ambled back toward the helm in an apparent sign of disinterest in the politics of sheep farmers and squatters. He was just interested in getting this stinking cargo out of the hold before it further fouled the already musty interior of his ship. He proceeded to steer the vessel in on its final windward run toward the sandy beach that stretched in a long sweeping curve from the small headland around the western edge of this part of the bay. He would have the crew furl the mainsail and slow to a steady drift to sound the depth here so as not to run her aground.

Taylor and Sutherland now busied themselves to get ready for the long trek overland that they had ahead of them which would start as soon as the sheep were unloaded. They had to carry their provisions while droving the sheep to the new run where further stores had already been set out and a hut built for their immediate and most basic needs by two shepherds already employed by the farmer. Taylor took care in unrolling a particularly long and heavy rifle that he had previously stored for the trip in a blanket roll. He also produced a pistol that he checked carefully, holstered and then threaded onto his belt.

****

Apart from a row of piled seaweed that lined the high-water mark, the beach where they landed the sheep was a narrow band of clean white sand. Looking to the south about three quarters of a mile distant was the small headland that the ship had sailed around earlier. To the north the water would have appeared to stretch to the horizon but for the imposing sight of the You Yangs rising up to define that end of the bay. The beach ran unbroken in that direction for a mile or two before bending out of sight to where there was a sort of bay within a bay. The smaller bay being known locally at that time as Jillong.

The water was of a clear light green colour over the white sand. It was clear enough to see an obvious drop-off from the shallows close to the beach into deep water only about 50 yards out. Well beyond this drop-off the ship was at anchor in a natural channel. The men could work here in the knee-deep shallows of the calm water to unload the sheep from the longboats onto the shore. The dunes along the beach here were very low and tea-tree scrub was scattered around a series of marshy ponds just beyond the low dunes. What was further inland from here these men had no idea.

Taylor and Sutherland were on the shore with their swags and equipment put in a pile ready to collect once the sheep were gathered ashore to begin immediately the trek north around the bay. Horses would have made their task infinitely less demanding however there was no way to land horses in the fashion that they were landing the sheep in this remote location so they would have to drive the sheep on foot.

The good thing about sheep is the tendency of the animals to gather in a herd. Cattle and horses on the other hand, while they too will congregate in herds generally, when scared or newly released will often bolt off in all different directions making individual animals very difficult to locate and regroup. A lesson hard learnt by the first settlers at Sydney Town who released cattle only to see them bolt willy-nilly into the bush, not to be seen again for some years. While it was expected here that the sheep would run a short distance once released on shore, they would gather in one large flock that could be easily rounded up by the two drovers and pushed off for the long walk north.

The sheep were clearly distressed. The long rough passage around Van Diemen's Land had taken its toll and this was now being compounded by the overcrowding in the unseasonably hot weather. They had not had food or water for some days, which was evident by the animals panting with mouths open and tongues lolling about as the crew unloaded them onto the beach. As a result, the sheep quickly scampered after one another through the low tea-tree scrub to the marsh in search of a drink. The men watched them go as they unloaded each small batch knowing that they would not go too far before joining the main flock where they would be rounded up shortly, when the unloading was complete.

From her elevated position on the hillside the young girl watched the sheep below milling about in the marshy area a couple of hundred yards away. From the family camp she, and her mother and father, had seen the large sails of the ship as it crossed backwards and forwards making its way into the wind where it eventually stopped off the beach. She had snuck down closer for a look at these strange furry animals that these new settlers kept bringing to the land in huge mobs. She had never seen men with sheep in this area though, only in the area to the very north-east of her lands. She giggled as she watched the sheep bounding down into the marshes chasing the main mob. The constant bleating seemed to her to be almost like some weird song.

She had left the camp without telling her father, as she knew what he would say. He always told her to stay well away from all these white fellas that were now spreading further and further around the land. If you spend time with a white falla, his spirit will make you sick, he would tell her. Even if you didn't see him do anything to hurt you, he will hurt you somehow. People rarely ever got sick in these lands for no reason before the white men started to arrive, unless they were old and dying, or someone "sung him" and deliberately made the person sick. Now people got really sick and many had already died just from going near the white fellas.

He had told her the stories of how white fellas had come along the coast in their wooden ships many, many years ago. Even as long ago as when her father was just a boy himself. He said that they came in ships to take the seals, and if given half a chance, would also take a woman. He said that stories from other lands told of the white fellas with their sheep taking more and more land while the owners of the land got sick and many even died during the invasion of their lands.

Buckley, her father said, had turned up after a visit to the bay from these ships. The girl knew the white fella Buckley. He was a very tall pale and slow man with a great long beard. The story was that at first he turned up carrying the spears that he had found of a recently deceased warrior. When the men first encountered this strange white figure walking up from the coast with their clansman's weapons, they thought he was the spirit of the man returned to walk amongst them. It soon became apparent, her father said, that he was just a big stupid white fella. The girl's people had looked after Buckley for many years although at times she recalled that he had left the people to live in his own hut. She had heard that recently Buckley had returned to the white people to learn to speak that language again and had left his hut and family.

As the girl watched the sheep for a while flocking in the marshes and around the low scrub, it become very apparent to her, even though she had hardly ever seen a sheep this close up, that they were distressed and becoming rapidly more so. She may not have known much about sheep but her experience of all the animals of her land gave her enough nouse to see that something was drastically wrong. Her elders had taught her all about animal behaviour as a matter of survival and she had all her life observed animals at close quarters.

Some of the sheep had now been unloaded for quite a while but the men could still be heard in the distance unloading from the ship and had not yet sought to round up the main flock. She moved down a bit closer to the marsh to see what was wrong. From her closer view, she saw that some of the sheep were staggering around and vomiting up water. Not just vomiting a small amount, but water gushed from their mouths like pouring water from a coolamon. Then she noticed that many had already collapsed but how many she could not tell for her vision was obscured by the low scrub around about where the sheep had gathered. The other sheep milled about bleating in anguish, perhaps fearing the same fate as those sheep lying about, some thrashing about, some laying still.

The young girl realised at once that there was a very good reason why these sheep were very sick, and possibly dying, they were guzzling down salt water from the ponds in the marshes. The sheep must have been extremely thirsty and had hunted out the first source of water that they could find. It may have been less salty than the sea, as these ponds would also collect some rainwater, but they were, the girl knew from experience, very salty to taste. At times of regular king tides the marsh would be flooded with seawater which was what created this series of ponds between patches of low scrubland. As she continued to move down the hill the girl witnessed that many of the sheep were around the ponds, drinking or showing signs of illness, and more were coming quickly in dribs-and-drabs from the direction of the beach. There must have been hundreds of sheep there now.

The hill that the girl walked down, descended gradually to the south to create just a small rise that divided these salty marsh lands near the beach, from a swamp that was fed by a small river that ran from the hills down to the bay. It was near this swamp that the girl's family had their camp. At this time of year there was plenty of fresh water with many birds including ducks and swans and also many swan eggs. These eggs were simple to collect for feasts and water birds that had never been frightened by guns were easy to hunt. It was to this swamp that the sheep should have gone to drink, as it was only a few hundred yards from the salty ponds over to that bountiful freshwater supply.

The girl did not think it through any further, her care for all things in nature and the sight and sound of sheep thrashing about dying before her eyes took over her sense of danger for herself. She bolted down to the area between the sick sheep and those still coming towards the ponds. In a half whisper, half yell, she told the animals to shoo away and directed the leading animals of that group toward the higher ground by waving her arms and jumping about wildly.

The girl found that by turning the lead sheep and running up and down the flank of the mob, they moved like one beast, like the way a flock of birds will all turn as one in flight, but nowhere near as elegantly, she thought. She became determined then, that if she could quietly get that main bunch moving in the right direction that the others would follow. The girl would then dart back to the hill and away from the white men before they knew anything about her intervention. She was pleased with herself at how quickly she had mastered the ability to handle the sheep and to save them from killing themselves in that horrible fashion of drinking the salt water. She smiled broadly as most of the sheep filed out of the scrub and over the small rise as she had directed.

****

On the beach, Taylor received a gruff farewell from the captain of the ship who was standing in a longboat being pushed off by the last of the crew to leave the shore. As they pushed the boat into the small waves the two crewmen jumped aboard the boat from either side and quickly took up the oars. Taylor thought he saw the captain chuckle to himself as he turned toward the bow as the boat was propelled back toward the ship. "He doesn't think we will make it", Taylor muttered to Sutherland and they picked up their belongings.

"Arrogant ol' bastard!" was all Sutherland said in reply.

These were not men inclined to great conversation. Taylor and Sutherland were hard men who said what they had to say and that was about it. They could live rough and work very hard for months on end. Both men had worked as farm hands in Van Diemen's Land and had gone to the mainland where they had the opportunity to be overseers of the new run. With shepherds and farm hands that they would now be in charge of managing. This was similar to the way that they had escaped poverty and unemployment in England when they left there as just boys for the guarantee of well-paid work that life in the new settlements of Van Diemen's Land had promised.

The two drovers both slung their blanket rolls across their backs, with food, water and a billy all bundled up together.

11

Taylor had taken out the rifle and carried that resting in the crook of his left arm. Sutherland found a stiff but whippy branch from under a nearby bush to use as a long walking stick and aid for shooing the sheep. Also, in the back of his mind, the stick would be handy if he came across the numerous and deadly snakes that he had heard so much about, that apparently inhabited the mainland areas.

They did not need to track the sheep in order to locate them. The noise that came from the main flock had persisted for the couple of hours that it had taken to unload all 800 sheep, ensured that Taylor and Sutherland had always been aware of what direction the sheep had gone and indicated that they could not have gone too far away. Taylor had led the way as the two drovers headed into the low tea-tree scrub to round up the flock and move them off on the journey north.

The girl jumped with fright and audibly gasped as the hand grabbed her elbow tight, with such strength that she could not move forward. She had been so absorbed in her labour of saving the sheep that she had lost all conscious fear of being discovered by the men who had left the ship and released all these sheep. "Jerri" her father's voice scolded her and put almost as much fear in her as if it had been one of the white men holding her arm. He was very angry with her. She had heard it in his voice and felt it in his grasp.

"Father, I was just trying to save these poor animals that are gorging on salt water and look" she pointed at the animals in catatonic states lying about the water holes, "they are all going to kill themselves!" She pleaded, looking up at her father's face with her big brown eyes. She spoke in the local aboriginal dialect of her people.

Her father stood tall and frowned down at the girl. He was a formidable sight, with his mop of shaggy black hair making him appear even bigger than he already was. His bare chest highlighted by the rows of scarring used to both decorate and to show he had been through his initiation when he was a boy growing into a man. The scars had been made by slicing the skin with a broken mussel shell to make a pattern of rows of short lines, that was then rubbed with charcoal or other materials to make the scars prominent and thick. Some men just had two or three single long scars, but Jerri's father had five full rows each consisting of many short cuts, making for a particularly impressive display.

He was a young man himself at the time and Jerri was his only child so far. As he always did when walking about, her father carried his waddie stick over one shoulder. A waddie was used as a weapon and also used for hunting and other things. The best waddie, her father believed, was the type that he carried. It was made by pulling up a small blackwood tree, the type that grew in the valleys of the ranges in the very south of their lands, roots and all. The sapling was then stripped of the branches and the fibres of the roots, and the trunk cut off at about three feet long and rubbed smooth all over with a hand-axe. This left a solid round head about the size of a man's fist at the end and a nice tapered handle. The waddie could then be further perfected by hardening the already dense timber over the fire and treating it with animal fats. This way a well-made and seasoned waddie could last for many years.

"Get back to camp now!" Jerri's father demanded. He frowned down at her, but his eyes kept flicking in the direction of the beach. "But father, can we just save this mob that I already…." She had no time finish the sentence before her father put his large hand on the back of her neck and moved her on in the direction of the hill. "Listen" he said "I will follow these animals and make sure they go over the rise to the fresh water, you head straight for the hill and the camp. Tell mother to pack for moving straight away." He darted off nimbly tailing the sheep as they filed out of the marsh. He was half crouching so that he was concealed behind the low scrub.

Jerri moved off quickly too taking rapid little steps with her head down with some feelings of shame for upsetting her father and causing him to come looking for her down here near the white men. She focused on the ground in front of her and wove her way expertly on bare feet through the tea-tree until she broke clear of the scrub and began to ascend the hill where this short adventure had begun. She did not look back in case her father saw her looking and accused her of dawdling.

"Holy Mary, would you look at that Harry!" exclaimed Taylor, as the men both saw together the mayhem that was revealed as they came through the scrub to the marshy ponds. There were many sheep strewn about in various stages of collapse and convulsion. Frothy water oozing from the mouths of some sheep that now lay still. "What the hell has happened to the poor bastards?" he exclaimed as though he were thinking out loud. Harry Sutherland had walked to the pond, kicking and prodding a few animals on the way, as if that was some legitimate method of diagnosis. "And where…" he paused to look around in a 360° arc, staggering back and almost falling over the carcass of a sheep in his horror, "are the rest of them?" he cried

While Sutherland poked around trying to figure out what had happened to the sheep, Taylor was close to a state of sheer panic. He had been charged with getting this flock to the new run. It was his chance to be the overseer of a farm far larger than most people back in England could even imagine. But, now the sheep were either keeling over by the dozen or had disappeared. The ship had sailed and they were on their own. This couldn't be happening to him he thought, he knew he had to get control of this situation or it was his balls that would be on the line.

Then as he paused to think, he had a moment of clarity. With a clear head his senses focused on the sound of the sheep. There was the bleating of the sick sheep around him in the scrub, and there was a second plane of sound. He realised that there was also the bleating sound of many sheep in the distance. He stretched up to his full height and scanned the rise beyond the scrub where he simultaneously caught sight of two scenes. The first was a row of sheep filing over the rise, and then disappearing out of sight. The second, the figure of a skinny black girl sneaking off up the hill to the right. *There* he thought, was his problem.

"Harry" he barked sharply, but not loud enough to alert the girl. Taylor motioned with his head and with a swift movement brought the rifle around to a position ready to quickly take aim if needed. Sutherland bounded back over the prostrate sheep to see what Taylor was watching. As he saw the figure of a young person walking up the hill just beyond the tea-tree Taylor had taken off through the scrub at a run in a half crouching position. "No, Taylor, stop!" he called, but all he saw was Taylor's tattered brown felt hat disappear from view as he ploughed on through the scrub.

Taylor quickly gained ground on the girl who walked despondently with her head down. Not hearing over the commotion of the woolly animals the running man who quickly approached. When Taylor reached the edge of the scrub he was only 30 or 40 yards from the girl who had her bare back to him moving directly away. Taylor's eyes were slits and his mouth a tight stretched grimace as he took careful aim through the iron sights of the rifle. As he focused on the girls naked back he could see the motion of her shoulder blades, the smooth muscles of her lower back and buttocks working as she walked uphill. The contour of her spine was in sharp relief with the side lighting from the afternoon sun. He took a long slow breath to steady his aim as he drew the sight on the middle of his target.

As the shot rang out and echoed around the hills, birds flew into the air in a sudden commotion and the sheep stopped bleating for a moment in apparent surprise at the treacherous blast of the gunshot. The sound that came to Taylor however was the roar of a man. The long and escalating cry that a soldier would make charging into the fray of battle. And when Taylor turned to his left in startled disbelief, that was pretty much what he saw through the cloud of smoke lingering from the discharge of his gun.

Coming toward Taylor at a rate of knots was a large black brute of a man almost totally naked with his arms raised above his head. His eyes were locked on Taylor's and his ferociously bared teeth were a gleaming white warning.

Although Taylor took little notice of the man's appearance, because his eyes were immediately focused on that formidable weapon that was clasped in the warrior's raised arms in clear anticipation of smashing Taylor's skull.

Taylor had nowhere to turn, he was caught out in the open and the man was bearing down on him too fast to even think about escape. The single-shot rifle was useless until it could be reloaded. Taylor could feel his heart pounding so hard his neck was throbbing with each pulsation like an artery was going to actually burst from the pressure. As the black man drew his arms back further to wield the waddie down on its ultimate goal Taylor drew the pistol from his belt and without time to aim blasted his assailant in the middle of his bare chest. The man's momentum sent him sprawling in a sliding mass of twisted limbs right to the feet of Taylor. Air and frothy blood bubbled from the man's lips with one last exhalation, and then he was still.

Chapter two

About ten years earlier Joseph Tice Gellibrand, who had been recently admitted as a barrister in London, after practising law for eight years, had set sail on a ship named The Hibernia with his father William for Van Diemen's Land. He was a young man of only 28 years of age at that time. A very young man, some would say, for the important position in which he was prepared to sail to the antipodes to take up.

At that time, the first Supreme Court was soon to officially open in Hobart and Gellibrand was to be the very first Attorney-General ever appointed to the position in Van Diemen's Land. In fact, the very first Chief Justice of that court in Van Diemen's Land, John Peddar and his family, were also sailing on the same Royal Navy ship as Gellibrand and his family. It was a distinct bonus for the young lawyer to be sailing with the judge as he and his father were able to become quite familiar with the judge and confident that the months of confinement on the ship were creating a mutually beneficial relationship between the two families.

Gellibrand and his family were already well known when they arrived in Hobart due to the reputation that preceded them from England. He was immediately accepted into the social circles of the elite and invited to dine and cavort with those who sought to be the influential class of the new settlements. The young Mr Gellibrand was also obliged to travel across the island colony to official appointments where he addressed the local dignitaries on the progress and importance of the new court.

Prior to the establishment of this new court in Hobart, all matters outside the jurisdiction of the local magistrate had to be referred to Sydney for hearing. The parties would have had to sail to Sydney and often remain there until the matter was finally resolved or otherwise adjudicated by the court. For matters referred to the higher courts the matter would actually be heard in London. This would be a very great inconvenience to all the parties indeed.

However, for all the benefits of the new court and legal advances for the colony, things did not stay so rosy for Gellibrand in this frontier legal society. After only one year his colleague Alfred Stephens, another even younger barrister, appointed as Solicitor-General to Van Diemen's Land had offered to resign rather than to continue to work with JT Gellibrand. He tendered his resignation to the Lieutenant-Governor, Colonel Arthur, with allegations that the Attorney-General was intimately connected to a vocal opponent of the Lieutenant-Governor and that he had engaged in unethical professional conduct.

It was suspected that Colonel Arthur may have been looking for the opportunity to pull the young Gellibrand into line given his associations with people seen as undesirables by the government for their open criticism of that establishment. Colonel Arthur was known for expecting his public servants to toe the line without question and would not have appreciated the autonomous activities of this particular Attorney-General.

Arthur did not accept the resignation of Mr Stephens. In fact, he directed Mr Stephens as Solicitor-general to turn his allegations into formal charges against the Attorney-general Mr Gellibrand. This was not such an easy process in a colony where the Court had only just opened, and there was no statutory tribunal or other body to deal with charges of professional misconduct by a legal practitioner available in Van Diemen's Land at the time.

With little other choice that he could see, the Lieutenant-governor directed that Chief Judge Peddar and two local magistrates form a board of inquiry, or commission, to investigate and hear the charges. This board was formed and began to hold meetings, but from the beginning Gellibrand was, naturally, not content with the proceedings. JT Gellibrand claimed the board did not have jurisdiction and was unconstitutional. He was also denied access to some of the documentation that he requested that had passed between Alfred Stephens and Colonel Arthur, further fuelling his animosity toward the Lieutenant-governor and the process of the inquiry in general.

The board continued with its inquisitorial mandate although not in open court, so it is not known exactly what went on behind closed doors. Various versions of the proceedings were reported by people involved or present for some, but not all, parts of the hearings. However, what is clear is that one day, when Gellibrand was once again frustrated at the way the proceedings were being conducted, he collected his papers, bid the board members good day, and walked out of the hearing. The end result of an adverse finding was from that moment on a foregone conclusion.

What Gellibrand had admitted to, and what the inquiry must have found, was that he had engaged in conduct that, at the very least, may be perceived as unethical conduct. While Gellibrand had practised law in London he had been retained as legal counsel by some ongoing clients, as any good and loyal legal practitioner would over the course of practice. Van Diemen's Land was at the time a small colony where most of the free settlers were coming out from England. As Attorney-general in those days he was permitted to undertake private legal work as well as government business. It came about that JT Gellibrand was, in his first year of office, given a brief to act for a party in a situation where he had already been retained by the other party in the same matter through the work he had previously undertaken in London.

Apparently, this was not that uncommon at the time, although it is clearly a situation where a conflict of interest arises. Gellibrand was pleading for both parties in settling some commercial matter, and of course one would expect that it would settle, where the legal representative knows the intimate details and respective positions of each of the parties. What Gellibrand should have done, was to refer the second party off to another independent legal practitioner, or at least exhausted all avenues to do so before agreeing to represent them.

After Gellibrand walked out of the inquiry, the report that eventuated was not released to the public. Sometime later Gellibrand himself published a small book on the matter setting out his version of what had taken place, with the lack of procedural fairness and impropriety in which he viewed the matter as vindicated by this board of inquiry.

The end result of this inquiry, set in motion by the Lieutenant-governor Arthur, was that JT Gellibrand was relieved of his duties as Attorney-general, after less than two years in the office. This must have been very embarrassing for the young lawyer who would have felt himself a big fish, in a very small pond in Hobart prior to these allegations being raised.

Although some might have thought it warranted, Gellibrand did not get struck off the roll as a Barrister and was free to continue his private practice as he continued to do following his dismissal as Attorney-general. But insult was then added to injury for young Gellibrand when he applied for a grant of land in Van Diemen's Land which was refused by the administration due to his conduct in the matters set out above.

So it was with this background that a few years later Gellibrand turned up as a key player in an association of colonialists with an extraordinary plan. This association came about when it had become well known among those on Van Diemen's Land that there were vast areas of land laying vacant on the mainland across the straight to the north of their island colony. While all the best farming land on the island had for the large part been allocated to private land holders, the administration of the mainland area of New South Wales was taking far too long to settle the south-east area of that territory. The association had an ambitious plan to take matters into the hands of its own members rather than wait any longer for government action.

The land in question had been known about and documented by explorers for some thirty years. Port Phillip was a large natural bay guarded by narrow rocky heads that fed into the straight due north of Van Diemen's land. This large bay made for an excellent sheltered harbour for ships with a deep channel running from the strait into the bay.

About 200 miles along the coast to the west of Port Phillip was another deep-water harbour known as Portland Bay. This bay had already become a base for the sealing and whaling ships that continuously worked this treacherous stretch of coastline where the prey for this industry could be found in abundance for those brave enough to pursue such a trade.

From what had been seen of the land in this south east corner of mainland New South Wales, there were thousands, or probably hundreds of thousands, of acres of grassy plains to the west of Port Phillip, and possibly all the way to Portland Bay. All that potentially profitable grazing land was then vacant and crying out to be settled and developed by the likes of those men who now made up this association.

So the association decided that rather than waiting for the colonial government to survey the land and to allocate land through land grants, they would draft a document, that would enable the Aborigines who lived on the land to sign that land over to the association. They could take up a vast area of land for agricultural use by some form of assignment from the traditional owners of the land, that would create a legal right that would circumvent the usual practice of land grants. What the association needed was a lawyer who would draft such a document, and for the task JT Gellibrand was their man.

Gellibrand drafted a document on behalf of the Association to obtain an interest in the land on behalf of the now one dozen or so colonialists, including Gellibrand himself, who had formed the company known as the Association and led by John Batman. This document, referred to as a treaty, had more the character of a leasehold, as there was to be an initial payment to the traditional owners, as well as an annual payment for the continuing lease arrangement.

Whatever one might think of this arrangement, for a private company to enter into a large-scale land deal with an Indigenous population, at least this association recognised that the Indigenous people had an interest and legal right to their land. This was more than the English Crown had ever done in its time on the continent. By offering even a token in consideration of the lease of the land by the Association made it clear that there was a legal right there worth acquiring. But this deal was not sanctioned by the colonial powers and was a very audacious and unprecedented foray into frontier colonisation that was bound to be nothing if not controversial.

JT Gellibrand had come to the colony as a very young barrister. He had attained the office of Attorney-general to Van Diemen's Land. He had been dismissed from that office in circumstances that amounted to dishonourable conduct for an office that should maintain such an air of high esteem. And now, Gellibrand was again at the forefront of what could only be described as an affair of highly questionable conduct, by the association as a whole, and particularly by the one providing the legal advice and drafting the terms of the entire deal. It was sure to attract the ire of the colonial administration once again.

And so Batman, the leader of the association, with a delegation of other members of the association and some Aboriginal men from another part of the colony met with some members of the local Indigenous land owners at Port Phillip. How these members of the local community were known to the association as the leaders, or had the right to act for the entire population of the lands in question is not clear. What is clear is that the Indigenous men who were present were not educated in matters of English culture and law, they spoke little if any English and could not read at all. The Aboriginal men who accompanied the association did not speak the local dialect and at best, may have had a few words of a common language, but nothing sophisticated enough to translate a complicated legal document. And even if they could, how could they convey legal concepts of assigning land rights to people who knew absolutely nothing of English legal concepts? Gellibrand, as legal counsel for the association would have been aware of all these factors that would mean that any contract in such circumstances would be found to be invalid and unenforceable at law.

****

Once Batman and several others of the Association had set up camps at the new port on the Yarra River in the Port Philip settlement, Gellibrand sailed north and visited the area. Once there he employed as his guide the convict man who had gone missing for 30 odd years and had lived with the local blacks of the areas west of what he had called the Yarra Yarra. William Buckley would have been invaluable as a guide in his knowledge of the country and his ability to translate for the local inhabitants. This was the land that Gellibrand had been told had some vast plains of untouched grazing land and he was keen to see what was on offer.

The association had sought to take the rights to the lands from the traditional owners and to divide that land amongst its members. The colonial government however was not inclined to recognise the validity of the treaty. What this meant was that the land remained Crown land and it would soon become public knowledge that the treaty claim failed. Every man and his dog would soon be clambering to the mainland to set up their own sheep runs as what were known as "squatters". The squatters would graze the land and set up homesteads so that once the government sent surveyors to allot crown land for farming, the occupier already having a farm on that land would have the best claim to the ongoing title.

Gellibrand had set off with Buckley and several other men to assist with camps on a south-westerly course from Batman's camp with a view to protecting these land claims. Buckley proved to know the area well however he frustrated Gellibrand in that for all his experience, he appeared a very dull and unintelligent individual. He could not, however, feel affected by his enthusiasm for visiting his friends in the tribes and his obvious delight at riding a horse for the occasion.

By midday on the first day of the journey Gellibrand and his crew arrived at the next main river to the west. At the time, being February and the height of summer, the river was not very substantial, but as it still flowed, and had cut out a significant ravine in the landscape, it appeared that it would be a reliable source of fresh water and must have run much higher at times of heavy rainfall. Gellibrand had been immediately struck by the beauty of the place. This was the river he had been told was named the Exe and was the source of water for the very selection of the Association's land that was set out to be Gellibrand's own run.

They turned their horses upstream and followed the high bank looking for a shallow place to ford this river, and also to find the area where the river water turned from salty to fresh. He sent three men downstream to find out how far inland from the bay they were so he could mark this on the charts he was preparing. The bank had smatterings of large gum trees with gnarly old trunks and thick canopies that were alive with bird life. Particularly a large white type of cockatoo with pink cheeks and a large curved beak that appeared as noisy, gregarious inhabitants of the space. The far bank had long grass that was at the time in seed and had gone brown in the summer sun. That grass appeared to thickly cover the plains that extended far beyond the other bank and extended for several miles to a row of high jagged hills or small mountains. This geographic feature of the landscape looked out of place, like it had just been plonked in the middle of the flat grassy plains. Buckley pointed out the high peak and told Gellibrand that it was called Wooloomanta.

Gellibrand followed the river upstream for a short distance until the river became a series of freshwater pools which satisfied him that it would serve the stock of a sheep run. While this land was to be his own under the terms of the Association's treaty, he was a very ambitious man and wanted to be certain that if he failed to gain the title to this land, he would have an alternative selection, or even a bigger and better selection, of land further west.

Once the men had all returned and eaten lunch by the River Exe, the party continued toward the area of Geelong. The high peak of Wooloomanta to their right and the bay to their left made for easy navigation and a gentle trek for the horses through the flat plains in between. Gellibrand however, found the heat of the midday sun extremely oppressive. At one stage he had insisted that the party stop and the men make a shade tent of a blanket for him to lay under for an hour or so to ease his exhaustion. He was glad of the supply of calomel pills that he had prepared for the journey just in case of such ailments or conditions and he took just three grains with water before resting.

The land out here was quite hard and rocky, and Gellibrand was less impressed with this land than that of the undulating fertile soils between the rivers where their journey had begun near the Yarra River. It appeared to be a soil largely of clay and would not carry as many stock in the drier months when the grass dried off even more than it was at the time he was there. They carried on at a gentle pace and soon came to another string of ponds where a great number of ducks and swans were observed. The fowl were not at all alarmed by the presence of the men and so two of the party took the opportunity to shoot a large black swan each. Buckley told Gellibrand that this area of land running down to the beginning of the bay known as Jillong, was called Lara.

Gellibrand was very appreciative of the cooler air coming off the bay and they made camp at a place overlooking the Jillong Bay. He rested again while the men set up tents and a fire for dinner and tea. The light south westerly breeze made for a very pleasant accompaniment to the satisfying meal made of the swans roasted over the fire with a billy of very sweet black tea. In the distance Gellibrand noted thin rising columns of smoke from other distant camp fires across the bay. While the party came upon many indications of native camps throughout the day, in the form of huts, implements and even a tame native dog, they had not seen a single soul so far.

"So William, why have we seen camps where the natives have been, but not one person all day?" Gellibrand inquired of his guide. The two men were relaxing, sitting side by side on the high point looking south across the bay in the twilight. There was little noise but the crackle of the small fire behind them, although the sounds of the numerous waterbirds carried a long distance across the water when they did cry out. The other men had hobbled the horses for the night and found their own quite places to recline leaving Gellibrand and Buckley in peace.

"Well sir, it's not that there is no one around. They knew we were coming long before we came by the camps. So in some places the people had just made themselves scarce, in others the camps were just not being used at this time." Buckley calmly stated. He continued looking out straight ahead, over the water. And in the profile of his weather-beaten face Gellibrand could see that on the native people, Buckley was proud and self-assured to speak about.

"Take that range of hills we passed today with the peak called Woolloomanta. That is a well sheltered place, overlooking the plains and easy to protect yourself. The clans would stay in that camp at times when the weather on the coast is bad, and when hunting on the plains and bush around there is good. Like for kangaroo and emu. Look at here behind us, where the freshwater pools of Lara are. Here the people trap fish at certain times of the year, so this camp would be used in that season. It is also a good place for yams when the roots are thick and easy to gather. In the warmer times, the people live near the sea and have camps set up there too. You can trap a lot of fish where the little rivers run out to sea you know. Best spot to have a base camp I reckon."

"So are you saying William, that the people don't roam from place to place, searching for food, as is the way the blacks are often described? I was told, that they have a sort of area where they were born, but they just move each time they run out of food. They leave everything behind and make a new camp where they find food again?"

"No sir! I have seen camps that are not that different to those I seen in books at school. The ones English people lived in hundreds of years ago. You know... in north England and the highlands of Scotland?"

"Hmmmm..." Gellibrand nodded slightly but had had a quizzical look of scepticism clearly on his face.

"The huts I have seen down on the coast, had stone walls,

only about so high." Buckley indicated about a foot from the ground with one of his large hands. "And then a pointy roof of sticks and reeds for thatching... That was pretty light, the roof part, but it could be easily rebuilt each year. That camp had an oven that everyone shared and a midden... do you know what a midden is sir.. a place where all the bones, shells and other scraps are chucked? Anyway, the earth oven and the midden there were so big, that camp must've been used hundreds of times. Every summer, over 'n' over by the generations, you know..?"

Buckley's expression had changed as the shadow of the thought that these generations of local custodians of the land were about to come to an abrupt end. He was remembering how he had seen firsthand how the settlers trashed the camps when they found them. Scattering the stone structures and looting the possessions from the camp. Even once by a whole wagon load. Presumably, the settlers did not want it to appear that the natives had substantial settlements, and perhaps they were aware that the scientific community back home in England had paid handsomely for such unique artefacts.

"The reason they didn't take their possessions with them sir," Buckley looked Gellibrand square in the eye, to emphasise this point, "was because they were their camps. No one else would ever go there, lest risk death if he did anyhow. And then next time they all returned to the camp next summer or whenever, all the stuff they needed was still there. You know, big grinding stones and the like."

Gellibrand was beginning to admit to himself that what Buckley had told him made perfect sense. The people were not nomadic, wandering blacks just following the trail of available food. They had set villages within their own tribal areas where they had stayed at particular times of the year, each and every year. Just like having a city house in London, and a summer house in Devon, he thought.

****

Gellibrand, with Buckley and the other men, had continued the journey around the area of the bay called Jillong and down the peninsular running south from there over several days. On the way back north, the group followed a large fresh-water river that wound its way inland and eventually curved away to the west. Buckley told Gellibrand of his previous sojourns far inland along that river course and of the hills, plains and lakes that existed in that area. But by then it had come to the time for the group to head north-east again to return to the camp of Mr Batman.

Gellibrand could not help but think that the land he had allocated himself from the Association land was quite inferior to lands he had seen on that trip, and maybe also to the land that Buckley had described further inland. Now that he had crossed his own land in the heat of summer, he came to realise that it was rocky and of clay base. Other areas, like the hills around the Yarra River, and the hills in this Geelong area also, had better topsoil and could retain moisture and pasture growth far better than that rocky ground could.

As they plodded along on the horses, making their way slowly back in the heat of the summer sun, Gellibrand asked of Buckley, "William, has any settler yet explored those areas you describe, west of this place? On these vast plains that you have told me about?"

"No sir!" Buckley exclaimed, without hesitation, "the lands of the local Barrabool Blacks ends at the west side of those hills there," he pointed to the hills back over his right shoulder. "And no one would dare enter the land of the next tribe. Like I said 'bout going into another man's camp. You risk death! We only went there at times we were 'specially invited for a big meetin'. A runner came around with a message stick once and we travelled to a big meetin' that only happens every few years on account of need'n to trade woman for wives. It is strict custom not to marry boys to girls that could be family. So sometimes girls had to be brought in from the next land, to add more girls to the clan that are not family. So that's was the only times we crossed that land"

Buckley paused and he thought for a minute about what he was about to say. Was Gellibrand open minded enough to understand the ways of the blacks? He decided being an educated man that he would not laugh at what he would go on to tell him.

"You see Mr Gellibrand, when the blacks talk about the risk of death, it is not the same as a white man like you means."

"Oh.." Gellibrand replied, as he glanced across at his riding companion.

"When a man dies 'cos he's been whacked with a waddie, or speared or somethin', well then he dies the same as a white fella. But, if someone dies for no reason of fightin' or nothin' then there still must be somethin'."

"I don't follow William."

Buckley struggled to find the words when speaking with Gellibrand. It was only 6 months since he started speaking

English again and he had not been that good at it to start with. "They are a pretty sound lot usually. They don't get sick much, sposen they got past being a baby that is. But they believe that by singin' a song at someone, or with other tricks, you can make someone get sick and die. Or, if you sneak into a land where you're not allowed to be, then the spirits of that land know what you did, and you will get sick and die. So you see what I'm sayin' 'bout risk of death? If you don't know nothin' 'bout diseases and such, then somethin' else has to account for the dying"

"Yes, I think I do understand William" Gellibrand said, thoughtfully he went on, "It is like any major religion I suppose, there are threats of dire consequences if one were to break the rules of the church."

"Well sir, it is a right mess now. See, for hundreds of years the people lived by this. If someone was sick only the spirit man of the clan could save 'em from dyin'. If a man broke the rules, another bloke might have to spear 'im, just in the leg like, to make things right again."

"So William, that sounds incredible, but let me see if I understand you rightly. A savage, of the same tribe, would spear another man in the leg. And by that retribution, save him from death by some sort of magic spirit trick?"

"Aye sir... dunno what ret'...ret'.... ret'bution is.. but that would make things right again. Seen it many times sir.... right with my own eyes!"

Both men had pondered on this for a few minutes, as the horses plodded on. The heat had been rising again and the flies becoming increasingly annoying. They seemed to love the smell of the horses and came in masses to buzz around the faces of the men and to gather in the corner of the horse's eyes. Gellibrand was again beginning to wonder how far he would get in the heat before he would have to stop for a cup of tea and to take a pill to recover his energy.

Buckley had continued. "It's all a mess now as I was sayin'. Now you have brought white man's diseases to the people. The blacks are getting' sick all the time and don't know why. White fellas have brought blacks from Sydney and Hobart that don't belong here. Black fellas from other lands are walkin' in to this country, without being asked, lookin' to get the blankets an' food that they're all hearin' 'bout. So you see. All the rules are bein' broke. It is very bad for me to see sir, what is happenin' to the people. Very, very bad."

Gellibrand did not respond to this further and Buckley rode on in silence. To Gellibrand, and all the other settlers of the time for that matter, this was progress and there was no turning back. The savages would have to get used to it or move on.

****

When the men got back to the camp at the mouth of the Yarra River, Gellibrand had camped in a large tent for a few days waiting for the ship to sail back to Van Diemen's Land. He also had to meet with some of the Association members to talk strategy, as it had become clear that the Colonial Government was not going to recognise their treaty with the natives. He had also asked Buckley to do something for him before he departed.

On the second night, Gellibrand had been sitting by a large communal fire at the camp site. In the twilight he watched the several ships anchored just off the point rock silently about in the light breeze that was always welcome in the heat of the summer. There was a mixed bunch of men at the camp and it seemed quite rowdy after his peaceful tour of the region. Some of the men were crew from the ships, some settlers waiting for stores, and some shepherds brought over to look after the many flocks of sheep now spreading across the lands. The men knew who Mr Gellibrand was, and they did not disturb this important gentleman unless he approached them first. Some of the groups of men had their own smaller fires in front of their own tents where they had sat on blanket rolls talking and drinking.

As he sat pondering a warm cup of sweet tea, he had seen the lumbering tall figure of William Buckley approaching in the glow of the flames. He was gesturing with his hand for Gellibrand to come aside and speak with him away from the other men at the fireside. As Gellibrand rose to move in the direction Buckley was moving he had noticed another shadowy figure hanging back and hesitating about coming into the light of the fire.

"Sir." Buckley half whispered as he met Gellibrand a few yards away from where he had been sitting, and in the shadow of the next tent. "I have found the man that can do the job for ye"'

"Good man. Good man William, who is he?"

"Well sir, he is one of the elders of the mob that are camped up on the river, on your run. But he has been doin' jobs down here for a bit of tucker, so he knows quite a bit of English.

The white fellas call 'im Jacky, but that ain't his real name 'course." Buckley said as they were both half turned looking at the figure holding back in the dark.

Buckley gestured to the man to join them, and he walked forward into the orange glow of the fire light and looked from Buckley's face to Gellibrand's as he walked up to meet them.

"Why he is not old at all," Gellibrand exclaimed as he continued to address Buckley and walked around the black man looking him up and down as thought checking out a horse that he may propose to buy, "for an elder I mean." Jacky was wearing the standard white breeches and red shirt that the Association had given to many of the black men, but his feet were bare. He stood there looking straight ahead at the fire while Gellibrand looked him over and spoke as though the man could not hear him. He was a tall man who stood proud and erect though his eyes did flicker to Gellibrand to see what he was doing walking about him.

"Well a black man can be considered and elder once he is a man. And these blokes don't often live to an old age like the folks back in England might. He is probably 25 to 30 years I reckon." Buckley had stated in a matter of fact fashion.

"Hello Jacky!" Gellibrand exclaimed in a firm voice, when he had finally stood in front of the man and looked him square in the eye.

Jacky looked down at the feet of the white man in fancy clothes, he had shiny shoes with silver buckles that looked ridiculous in the dusty bush camp. "Hello mister." Jacky said quietly, not looking up again.

"Mr Buckley tells me that you come from the land around the river west of here?"

"Yeah, mister." Jacky continued to look down at the ground.

"And he has told you that I want you to look after that land for me. And not to let anyone else run their sheep there?"

Jacky looked up, and then turned toward Buckley, with a helpless look on his face.

"He dun' 'stand English that well sir, but I told 'im what you said, that only Mr Gellibrand and his men can run sheep on that land." Buckley said as he came forward to join the conversation, then he said a few words Gellibrand could not understand to the native, and Jacky then nodded enthusiastically. "And he gets what it is he has to do."

"Good. Very Good Jacky. If you look after the land for me, I will look after you and your family so you can learn how to live like a real farmer too!" Gellibrand paused and looked unconvinced at Buckley. "He does understand that, doesn't he.... he needs to know that in the long-run, he will be much better off?"

"Yes, yes. With all that is going wrong for these fellas, he was very happy to know that you want 'im to stay on that land. He knows that you will be back after the cold season to start bringin' stock ont'a the land, and he gott'a look after that place 'til then." Buckley said, and Jacky had continued to nod in apparent agreement to all that was being said.

"Righto then chaps, just wait here a minute then." Gellibrand stated and he lightly stepped across to where his own tent was and he ducked inside. Buckley and the native man looked at each other, wondering what was going on.

Gellibrand emerged again carrying something in his hands like a page boy carrying an offering to the alter. He presented, laying across both palms of his hands, to Jacky a large knife. The knife had a handle that was part of a deer antler and the long blade was covered within a leather sheath.

"Go on, take it, I won't bite you!" Gellibrand goaded. Jacky picked up the knife in his left hand by the sheath, and his right hand he moved to slowly wrap around the handle. It had felt like a fine fit within the palm of his hand as the curve of the antler suited the grip well. He extracted the blade from the sheath. The blade was about 6 inches long and not perfectly even in the taper and dull in appearance, as though it had been hand forged. It was however, a skilfully crafted and almost indestructible hunting knife that Gellibrand had carried with him from England. Jacky gazed at the blade with wide eyes as he turned the blade over and over, reflecting the firelight as it revolved.

"Now that is yours to keep Jacky, and there will be much more for you and your people if you do right by me." Gellibrand stated, in his most magnanimous voice. Buckley said something to Jacky, who still looked spellbound at the knife. He quickly reinserted the knife into the sheath and tucked the whole thing into the back of his dungarees.

"If that is all Mr Gellibrand, Jacky is wantin' to get back now?" Buckley said, and Jacky looked around with a slight nervous look at the other men around the camp.

Gellibrand said goodbye to his newest agent on the mainland and Jacky and Buckley walked slowly away from the camp while they chatted animatedly in a language foreign to the Englishman's ears. Gellibrand walked back to the main fire and beckoned all the men to come and listen to something he had to say. A murmur went through the camp as word passed around between the groups of men.

When the majority of the men from the camp had gathered in the light of the main fire, Gellibrand stood up on a log so as to address also those standing behind the men still seated around the fire. The men shuffled about, some muttering to each other, most had a cup in their hand of either rum or tea. Mostly rum.

"I just wanted a quick word with you men." He called out loudly, in his best bar-table voice, "I think most of you know who I am but in case you do not, I am Joseph T Gellibrand, one of the founders of this settlement and lawyer for the Association." The he paused for comments, but there were none, as he had expected. "Some of you men will also be looking to settle in this land yourselves, and others among you will be running the sheep of other settlers. As you also know, it seems that the Colonial Government, for God only knows what reason, is not recognising the treaty that has been duly executed with the local savages. Do not! I repeat: Do not, my friends, think that this extinguishes the claims to the land that each member of the Association has validly made, and each allotment is clearly set out on the map that Mr Batman has, should anyone wish to inspect it. As soon as the Governor appoints a Crown Land Surveyor to this settlement, those allotments will be submitted to the Governor and no doubt will be granted to the association members as planned."

Gellibrand rocked on his heels while he looked about the faces of the men, and as he also expected, no one had challenged his authority to make such claims. He smiled inwardly as he went on "You will all know that the general areas of the claim are from the River Exe just to the west of here, east across the Yarra Yarra area and right up to the hills in the east and north. Also, the area known as The Peninsular from the bay known as Jillong right down to the heads of Port Philip."

"What are we 'spossed to do with all our boss's sheep when the only place they offload 'em is either here, or on the heads?" A scruffy looking Sheppard, standing just at the edge of the firelight called out over the heads of the other men. A few other men murmured to each other in response and heads then turned back towards the man standing tall on the log.

"Thank you my friend, that is a very good question and something I also meant to raise with you all." Gellibrand continued, with his chin held high as he paused again until he had everyone's eyes looking at him once more. "I urge you, who have taken charge of sheep that do not belong on any of the current allotments to take your flocks to the area west of here known as Lara, or to some people as The Duck Ponds. This area is between here and the Jillong Bay, it has good water and feed, and is a fine location from which to strike out to your lands once you have orders on where to take the flocks. There is plenty of space there to keep the flocks separated and to wait with your sheep. There is no excuse to go and start grazing stock on lands that are already allotted to those settlers who have existing claims."

Gellibrand waited for a few moments on the log and looked around across the faces of the men. The men had just looked at each other or at the ground. A few had started to shuffle off while muttering away to each other. No one spoke or challenged Gellibrand further on what he had said. The men who had been sitting around the fire drifted back into their previous rowdy conversation. A sailor spouted boastful stories of adventures had in other lands while swinging his cup of rum with such animation that waves of the brown liquid had sloshed over the sides. When Gellibrand stepped down he was content to sit back down and he resumed his place as a passive participant in the fireside gathering.

Chapter three

Jacky and his clan had maintained their camp on the Exe River over the Autumn as planned. A wave of illness had gone through people and as many as half their number had died from the disease that came with the white man. As they did not then have as many people to feed there had still been plenty of food in the area to sustain them, supplemented also with the food that Jacky brought back when he went to the settlement to work unloading the ships. He had preferred to stay with his family when there was no work to do at the settlement. He had a young wife and she wanted to have a baby, but in such uncertain times, Jacky had urged her to hold off.

Jacky had been thinking about this as he watched his wife Murnin bathing one of her sister's little boys down at the edge of the river. Jacky sat cross legged at the top of the riverbank in the shade of a large gum tree, where he had a view of the women at the river and could also see out on the plains to the west to keep an eye out for the return of the young men who had gone hunting that day at dawn. He was carefully sharpening his new hunting knife on a grinding stone in anticipation of being the elder who would be charged with dividing the animal among the various family members, according to their rank in the community, once the hunters returned. The rock on which he had slowly worked the blade had a groove made deep on the surface from many years, or centuries, of men grinding stone axes in much the same way.

The young boy had giggled and pulled to get away from the beautiful young woman, just a girl herself then really, who held him by the wrist and poured water over his leg. He danced around in the ankle-deep water as the cool water excited his senses.

"No auntie, no!" he cried between laughs as he pulled harder to get away.

"You must let me clean this cut Barat, and keep still with me until it dries so that I can cover it again with fat." She said in a soothing voice as she smiled at the little boy and kissed him on the forehead.

Jacky smiled to himself as he watched this happy exchange, but he soon thought to himself how rare it was becoming to see any woman of his people with a happy infant to take care of in this way.

Chapter four

Gellibrand sailed back to Van Diemens Land to get back to his usual business as barrister and, to a lesser extent, his work in editing a small local newspaper in Hobart. He had then fresh in his mind how much of a fortune there was waiting for the adventurous type on the mainland with so much unoccupied grassland. He had planned to use his status to exert influence in the colony to continue to push for the Associations right to the land around Port Philip and to dissuade those not members of the association from trying to jump in and squat on the land before any system of land grant could be implemented. He would also use his more covert influence as a newspaper editor and regular anonymous contributor to criticise the Governor and to undermine any policies that went against his interests, or those of his associates.

When he had resumed his rather privileged lifestyle back in Hobart he remained vigilant of developments on the mainland and remained hopeful that Jacky was looking after his then vacant sheep run. He also hoped that the speech of warning he had given to the men at the dock before he left had made an impression on them that they would heed and use the Lara pools as a holding place for grazing flocks and not camp on his land.

He had spoken with his father at length about these issues and together they decided that JT Gellibrand would immediately plan his next trip to the mainland to secure the run and to get some sheep onto the property. Gellibrand also told his father about the vast plains of land that stretched from the river near Jillong Bay out to the north and west as far as the eye could see. Land he told his father that was superior to that of their existing run and was at that time still completely unoccupied. His father had warned him to take things one step at a time, and not to trust the care of the run to the savages who, in his view, would just wander off and leave it as soon as it suited them. William Gellibrand suggested that JT should take his own son over to the mainland on the next expedition as he was by then himself a talented young man.

Chapter five

Jacky had seen the man approaching from the west in the warm winter sun of the early morning. He carried three long hunting spears in one hand and shielded his eyes with the other. Looking for their camp. He was dressed only in the traditional belt of feathers and fur and he walked boldly across their land, but was not one of its people. Jacky had known that the man was coming when still a couple of miles out, as the young men hunting in the morning had already covertly marked his arrival on the land from a distance. Most likely a boy carrying a message stick they had assumed. But as he had come closer, they could see that he was a tall fit looking man of about Jacky's own age. The man walked nimbly across the broad plain on bare feet between the tufts of grass and occasionally he had disappeared from sight into the deep shade of a one of the numerous large old gum trees.

Jacky rose and walked out to meet the man who was converging directly on the camp with the smoke from the cooking fire wafting softy up above the river red gums. The man, as a skilled hunter, may just as easily have been following the numerous footprints of the inhabitants leading always and inevitably back home. Jacky waited in the open sunlight with his waddie held in both hands across his chest like a soldier would hold a gun. A small gathering of curious spectators, mostly children, milled about in the shadows behind him wanting to get a look at a rare visitor to the land.

"What are you doing here, without being invited to the land?" Jacky asked as the other man stopped a few paces away. The men examined each other carefully. Jacky could see the obvious scarring of an initiated man of a similar type and pattern to that on his own chest. The man looking Jacky over however, saw a man in a traditional setting, but wearing full clothing of a dull red shirt and light dusty pants.

The man looked at the ground at Jacky's feet after each had taken stock of the other, "I seek welcome to the land of my brother, the Wautherong, and pay my respect to the elders." He stole a glance at Jacky's face to gauge the response but got no indication. "I ask only to pass your land for time enough to see the white man that gives away the steel axe, rugs and food."

"You should not have come here. The white men are bringing nothing but trouble. They are bringing people onto land already that do not belong here. People are getting sick and dying from some spirit that is not of our land. You should respect the ways of your own elders and go back to the lake country from where you came."

"Please let me cross your land. One of my own aunties is Wautherong and I ask you as a brother to let me onto your land. My family too have been sick and some have died with a skin sickness since the white man has been in the area, on your lands. We are suffering too, but not getting any of the things that you got from them. You have the dress of a man I have never seen and I am sure that you have taken the other benefits or you would not let them stay on your peoples land?" The man continued to look at the ground with a pleading disposition and expression of genuine unified intentions. His right hand raised and resting on the shafts of his spears, his other hand held at waist height with the palm up.

Jacky was aware that at times some women had been exchanged for wives with the people from the lake country to the west. It was therefore likely that it was true that this man could have had an auntie from the Wautherong people and that he was a relative. But generally these people were their enemies and they would protect the lands at all costs from any invasion. What he also knew was that these were unprecedented and very strange times. The invasion of the white settlers had created far greater problems for everybody than one man crossing onto their land uninvited. He could not help but feel for the man and his circumstances.

"Come on, he said, if you are going to be welcomed you had better come and meet with all the elders."

The man from the lake country sat in the shade of the tree with the other men. He told them that his name was Tanapia. The women and children pretended not to watch as they went about their business gathering food and firewood along the river banks. He told them of his family and people of his lands. That he was from the Colaknat Lake tribe that was several days walk from the river that bordered the western edge of the Wautherong land. Some of the older men knew of the lakes as they had participated in large ceremonial gathering with these people themselves some years ago. They all shared in the reminiscing of the family ties that existed between the two groups and they all laughed when they figured out that the two men were in fact cousins of some sort. The men brought him cool clear water to drink and later he shared the evening meal with the men around the main fire and settled in for the night, comfortable that he had been accepted, at least temporarily, into this river community.

The people became quiet and drifted off to separate huts and shelters spread about for the family groups. There were still bursts of chatter, too soft or too distant to be intelligible by the visitor, but he thought it may have been and extra layer of flutter due to his arrival in the camp. Someone tossed the man a rug to sleep under for the cold night air had crept into the camp and the fire burnt down to orange glowing coals, fanned brighter occasionally by the soft breeze following up the river basin. The sounds of the river birds and the croaking of the frogs seemed to become louder and louder when the people were all gone.

This rug he was given was nothing like the rugs he had seen before. His own rug at home was made of possum skin and was thick and very warm. It was decorated on the skin side with many line drawings that set out stories or reminded him of characters from stories, or the many animals and animal tracks of his area. Things he had learnt as a child and it served to remind him and to aid him in teaching the youngsters of the new generation. His rug was built and added to over the years, repaired and treasured as the most important garment a person ever owned as was particularly evident in the cold wet weather that seasonally occurred in this southern land. It was cold enough now, but the real wet windy weather of winter was a while away yet. He leaned forward toward the remnant fire to get some light and he turned this new rug in his hands.

It was grey and soft but smooth and not with fur like his possum skin rug. It was completely even with no joins, like it was cut from one great big skin, but it was the same on either side. It must be like the material that made up the clothes that some of the men in this camp wore he concluded. He cast the grey blanket about himself and laid down beside the fire. He looked up at the same stars that he saw every night at home, and listened to the same sounds of the water creatures that he heard by his own lake. As he drifted off to sleep he wondered how long it would take for him to achieve his purpose, and slip back to his own people, who awaited his return, camped just the other side of the territorial boundary.

****

In the morning Tanapia spoke with Jacky again, about a visit to the white-mans' camp.

"Can you take me to the white fellas who give out the steel axes?"

Jacky looked at the man with an expression of genuine concern. "Yes, I can take you there." He paused for a few seconds, watching the children playing below their position on the riverbank. They yelled and chased each other along the edge of the water, those being chased squealed in delight at the risk of being splashed by the ice-cold water. "But I warn you not to get involved. They are already on our land, and on the land of the Yarra Yarra where they have the big camp. We have to try to get along with them, so that we can share the land. They have many animals, food in big bags that they can carry around, weapons like nothing that you would have ever seen. I have made a deal with the man who will share this land with us, to let his animals eat the grass and wander here. He will give us protection and food and other things when we need it. I had to do this for the sake of all these people" He gestured around him with his hand and looked again at the children playing in the warmth of the morning sun. "I have to be the one who works with these men, because to go against them would mean a war that we could not win."

Tanapia looked down at the ground in front of him. He scratched at the dry ground between his feet with a stick where they sat again beneath the large river red gum. "Aha, well why don't you move back in your land away from them. Leave the Yarra Yarra and this border land to them, use the country your people have back in the bush?"

"It is not that easy cousin. There are men who are already moving out onto all areas of our land. There is nowhere left for us to be on our own. We can't run away, we have to work with them. You are still able to get away and maybe they will not take their animals as far as your lands in the lake country, as it is too far away from the main camp that they have now. Anyway, they will not just give you things today if you go and see them. You have to do something for them, or be like me, and let them share your land."

"Well I have heard of others who come and get things. I just want to get what I can, and then I will go back to my land, as far from these white men as I can get. Please help me do this and I will leave you in peace."

"Look, my brother here has been going down and helping

them unload the ships."

"Unload ships..." Tanapia repeated back, with a puzzled look on his face.

"You will see when we get there. Help out doing that for a couple of days and they will give you some of the things you want. He will help you because you can't speak their language." Jacky stood and buttoned up his red shirt, brushed the dust and dry leaves from his trousers with his hands. "Come on then!" He said, as he gestured with his hand for the man to get up from the ground.

Jimmy was the name the white men had given to Jacky's brother. He was a few years younger than Jacky and always appeared generally happy and care free. He let Jacky do the worrying about dealing with the camp, the people, the white men or whatever. He bounced along with a smile on his face as the three men walked together along the river bank towards the bay.

They did not speak much. This was all new land to the man from the lake country, and it was very rare for someone to leave their traditional lands. At home, Tanapia knew every creek, hill, lake and plain that he crossed, and had been crossed, by his ancestors for thousands of years. It was a very strange feeling for this man to walk across foreign land. He was taking it all in and experiencing a strange sense of awe. They crossed the river so that they could head east toward the main camp at the port. From here the men began to see signs and tracks that Tanapia had never seen before. Large hoof prints of horses, long parallel lines pressed in the sand from wagon wheels and the tracks of men wearing boots on their feet. Soon they saw and heard the first herd of sheep, and in the distance, what was fast becoming a village of huts and tents. Jacky noted that on the hill north of the river a bigger and more permanent settlement was appearing around the house that had recently been built for the man named Batman, who was the main leader of the men here.

As they walked into the port camp, Tanapia was almost overwhelmed looking everywhere at so many foreign things. There were men coming out of white canvas tents, dressed in clothes like those that Jacky and Jimmy wore, wooden barrels stacked about, unusually coloured dogs chasing each other about and in the distance ships. Tanapia had heard about ships, and seen them from a long distance from the cliffs on the coast at home. Here there were a number of ships, some anchored out in the bay, two tied up to a roughly constructed wooden pier. As they walked towards the pier the men were aware of many eyes upon them, as white men, black and brown men, paused in their work to watch them pass by.

At the pier Jacky recognised a large well-dressed Englishman standing out on the pier barking orders at men who were on the deck of a ship. Jacky walked up to the man and the other two men followed. He addressed the large man in a language Tanapia did not understand. "Mr Smith, my brother and this man are looking for work for today. This man is Tanapia and he wants a steel axe and some blankets if you can spare them for his help?"

The big man stopped what he was doing and regarded the three men before him. He had a coiled rope draped from his right hand and he slapped the coil against the stiff cloth of his black trousers as he thought about this proposal. He looked at the near naked black man and wondered how on earth he got around like that when it was cold. The three men stood looking down before him. Jacky looked up and held a hand above his eyes to shield from the sun to see if he was going to answer.

"Yes, alright Jacky" he said "Tell 'em to get down into the hold and to pass the goods up to the men on the deck." He looked Jacky in the face to see if he was comprehending, he assumed that he was, "And tell 'em that we have that other ship to unload yet, so there is a couple of days work if they want it." He gestured with his thumb over his left shoulder at the other ship. The men on the deck of the first ship had stopped to watch what was going on, "Get back to work you lot!" He barked again the men jumped and busied themselves, "And you blokes get to it!" he said to the new recruits as he turned to walk back off the pier.

Jacky knew this man Smith from his previous visits to the camp and he knew that like Gellibrand, he was bringing loads of goods and stock to the land to set up his own large runs. He seemed to be a powerful man by all the goods that he possessed, his clothes, and the way even men like Gellibrand regarded him as though he were a respected elder of these people.

As Smith walked off the pier he became aware that Jacky was walking off behind him also. He stopped and turned, "So why aren't you lookin' to work as well Jacky?"

Jacky had almost run into the man when he stopped in front of him and turned, he looked at him almost toe-to-toe. He could smell the foul smoky breath of the large man looking down at him. "I just work for Mr Gellibrand now," he said, glancing quickly up at the eyes of Smith.

"Oh, is that right is it?"

"Yeah, I look after his land for 'im while he is not here. He said that if I do that, when he starts his run, we will be like partners."

"Ba ha ha.." Smith guffawed loudly right in the face of Jacky, who stepped back and looked down at his feet. A couple of other white men passing carrying large sacks over their shoulders sniggered openly at the scene as well, although they hadn't even heard what was said. Smith hooked his thumbs into the straps of his braces and he continued to chuckle while slowly shaking his head from side-to-side. "You really think that a wealthy city gentleman like Mr Gellibrand would have a black fella like you as a *partner*!" He laughed out loud again and put his hand on Jacky's shoulder in a consoling, but condescending motion. Then in a voice loud enough to ensure that the passing men did hear this time, he went on "He might let you shovel the horse shit out of his stables, or let your daughters warm the sheets of his bed, but Jacky, you will never, ever, be a partner to an English gentleman!"

Smith took his hand from Jacky's shoulder and turned while still laughing dramatically, to the point where he had to put his hands on his knees and take a deep breath to regain his composure. The men around had stopped working and looked at Jacky and laughed aloud as well, passing sycophantic glances to Mr Smith.

Jacky turned with his head down to walk away. He looked out at the ship to see if his brother and Tanapia were watching his humiliation, but thankfully it appeared that they had already descended into the hold of the ship and did not see.

He slinked away quickly between the tents and avoided the looks and muttered comments of the men in the camp. He knew that he had to trust Gellibrand and that to do a deal with the white man was the best way, in fact the only way, to ensure a future for the people about whom he cared the most. He had felt the blood rise to his face at the insults of Smith, but he had to maintain his dignity and be the better man.

That night, the men and women at the river camp ate separately as usual. Jacky had been troubled by what had happened at the port today as he sat reflecting the event in the coals of the fire that he sat around with the other elders. Jacky got up and looked at the sunlight fading and the western horizon was bright orange, fading to purple and a brilliant blue above that. There must be bushfires somewhere way off to the north or west, he thought, creating the haze that elicited such brilliant sunsets. It reminded him that greater things still go on, much greater than that what had happened to him today, the natural way of the land would continue no matter what men say. He went and found Murnin with the other women, by the river, he took her hand without speaking, she rose and he led her up the path along the bank.

After they made love, on the soft bed of trampled green reeds by the edge of the water, he lay on his back looking at the stars that were filling the twilight sky above. A mosquito buzzed in his ear, attracted by the hot breath and sweat that filled the air about them both but he was too relaxed to move. She lay on her side and had her left hand resting on his chest, and her head on his shoulder. She sensed that his body was at ease, but his mind was still spinning.

"What is it?" she asked, without moving to look at him.

"I don't know if we should be staying here. Maybe we should be staying well away from these white men, and bringing up the children in the same way we were?" He let out a deep sigh and her head rose and fell with his chest, "But where can we go that is not now already within their reach?"

She rose her head slightly to look at him. The camp down the river was quiet now but the sounds of the river were getting louder as the darkness increased. Frogs croaked so close to her that when she moved her foot one fell silent instantly. "I know that you are a good man. I know that what you are doing is entirely to take care of the future for all of us."

"Hmmm..." was all he said, he did not meet her eyes.

"You are a clever man. To learn the language of these men and to be able to make a deal with them shows you are a great leader. No one else here has been able to achieve so much." She also laid back and looked up at the stars for a while. He still did not speak again, but she knew he was still thinking. "I have been thinking though, of what will become of our first baby, in this time of such great change. Some of the other women are saying they will not raise babies at this time, it is too uncertain what will become of them, and who will be left to look after them? So many people sick, dying and having their land taken over."

"Yeah." he said as he rose and bent to take her hand "It's getting cold". He helped her to her feet and together they walked back to camp in silence to sleep for the night in their little hut beneath their thick possum skin rugs.

****

Gellibrand and Hesse

It was two days since Jacky had left his brother and the man from the lake country, Tanapia, at the port unloading ships. He removed his rug, that he wore like a cape against the cold wind and dressed in his clothes and after a morning meal he headed off alone down the river, for the now familiar trip onto Yarra Yarra land to the main white man's camp. Since the autumn rain the grass and young wattles had grown quite thick along the river, as they did at this time of year. Mr Gellibrand would be pleased to see the land in this healthy state he thought as he picked his way around the vegetation. He must ask Gellibrand for boots when he gets back this time too, he thought, as he stepped into a patch of bog and the black mud oozed up between his toes. He also found that he had to get wet almost to his waist to cross at the usual place, as the river had risen due to more rain in the hills to the north. He made a mental note to find a place further upstream to cross on the way home where there a more shallow sand bars so he wouldn't have to get so wet and muddy again.

He wanted to get to the port in time to return to his river camp by dark. Jacky hated having to stay for any longer time in the port camp than he absolutely had to, he always preferred to be back on his own land with his people safe around him. He hoped that the ships had been unloaded and the men would be ready to return with him by mid-afternoon as the sun was setting earlier each day at this time of year.

The sound of the laughing and men's voices carrying on meant that Jacky did not have to look far for his brother. He could hear his well-known laughter and chatter before he even reached the edge of the camp proper. At a tent on the path towards the port there was a small camp fire burning. A few scruffy white men sat on upturned wooden crates around the fire, chatting and laughing, with bottles of rum in their hands. One man played a lively tune on an accordion. Jacky's brother and Tanapia danced around like court jesters before the white men, jiggling around on their long slender legs and making strange sounds neither Jacky nor the other men could understand. They each had a tin cup in their hands. This was a camp where the woodcutters supplied firewood to the port, cut from the stand of eucalypts growing around here. There were fallen logs and stacked split wood piled nearby. Also this was a popular place for the working men and sailors to come and get drunk away from the judgemental gaze of the bosses and gentlemen in the main camp.

It was apparent that the men had finished unloading the ships and were enjoying the rewards for their labour. In fact, it was not unusual at that time for the workers to be paid, at least in part, in rum, rather than wholly in the scarce currency of the colony. When the accordion music stopped, the two aspiring clowns held out the cups for the appreciative audience to pour nips of rum into, which they did in liberal streams from their near full bottles. They sipped from the cups, giggled like children and returned to sit on the ground in the circle with the other men. That was when they saw Jacky standing back watching, with a look of disgust on his face. Everyone around the fire was quiet and had registered the stern look on the approaching black man's face. Except for one particularly drunk young sailor, who held out his bottle and called "Hey fella! You wanna dance too, we got more rum... heh heh heh.. an' it only takes a couple of nips for yous blokes to be pissed!"

Jacky ignored him and addressed his brother and Tanapia directly in their language. "Have you got your things? We are going."

"Aww. Come on brother, sit down and rest for a minute!" his brother slurred at him, waving the tin cup before his face before taking a long slug of the strong and horrible tasting liquor. Jacky took the cup from his hand and threw it aside, spilling the small amount of residue on the grey earth. The white men looked from Jacky, to the cup, and back again. All apparently well inebriated to a point not to care enough to take much interest in the black fella relations. Jacky walked a few yards from the group with his back to them and waited for his brother and Tanapia to follow.

On the way back to camp, Jacky walked at a deliberately fast pace. The other two men hobbled along, racing to keep up. Tanapia now had a pair of pants on, and in a belt fashioned out of a strip of canvas had tucked a small steel axe with a wooden handle. A standard grey blanket was also draped around his shoulders. He looked very uncomfortable, and paused frequently to pull up the pants, and adjust the belt and axe. His squirming around with his pants was almost as ridiculous as the dancing he was doing around the fire. Jacky was unrelenting however, he stared straight ahead and kept up the quick march away from the port area and back to the river.

When they struck the river about three hours later on the usual path, Tanapia and Jacky's brother knelt beside the water and splashed the cool refreshing water on their heads and rinsed the foul taste of liquor from their now very dry mouths. Jacky was glad that the foreign man now had his possessions of an axe, blanket and pants and would be able to leave them again in peace with just his own people.

"Keep going," Jacky said, nudging the leg of his brother with his toe and turning to head up-river.

"Just let him rest for a while, the camp will still be there tonight" Tanapia said, looking Jacky straight in the eyes in a look of defiance.

"We need to find a better place to cross the river upstream, I don't want to be looking for one in the dark. You can rest here if you want, we are going on."

Jacky's brother got up and obediently followed with his head turned down and his arms hanging limply at his side. Tanapia paused until the men were disappearing into the bush, then he rose, sighed loudly, and quickly followed as well.

The three men followed the flat land above the river valley and had only walked maybe half a mile upstream when they heard the rhythmic sounds of an axe cutting wood start abruptly in the almost silent bush. A few birds fluttered back over their heads startled by the sound and Jacky stopped instantly in the way that a hunter freezes mid-stride when he sees prey that has turned toward him. The other two men also froze silently behind him, each tilting their heads to identify the direction of the origin of the sound. They turned to exchange glances when they also heard the distinct call of men as the wood chopping sound had abruptly ceased. White men were working somewhere beyond the trees directly in their path and not far ahead.

Jacky motioned almost imperceptibly with his hand for the others to follow and he stalked on silently. He walked slowly and rolled his feet very deliberately on the outer edge of his soles so as not to make a sound and to detect dry leaves and twigs beneath his feet before they could crack. This silent stalking was a necessary skill that these men possessed through years of staking animals, and each was a master at the art.

As they came to a break in the trees the scene opened up before them. In a clearing within about 100 yards of the river two men were constructing sheep yards. One man was closer to them, he had several long poles cut from the bush and he was using a large axe to shape the end of the poles. The other man was setting posts in place in the ground. He had a pipe in his mouth and regular large puffs of smoke were drifting from beneath his broad brimmed hat and vanishing into the soft breeze.

Jacky crouched down to take in what he was witnessing here not very far from his own river camp. The men had cleared a few trees and with the cut bush poles were constructing a small holding pen. To his left Jacky could see a rough wooden hut, covered with the canvas like the tents at the port. To the right a track led away west where horse and wagon tracks could be seen in the damp ground. There were no animals yet in this clearing, however it was obvious that they were getting ready to bring stock into this land. Jacky was disappointed with himself for letting this camp get set up so close to his own camp without him even noticing.

When he turned to speak with the other two, he was hit with the alcohol fumes of their breath as they crouched close in the undergrowth. They now looked bright and alert in their eyes though, evidently excited by this new discovery. "I've got to speak with these men, they can't camp here if they are not Mr Gellibrand's men." He looked from one face to the other as he spoke in a whisper. They did not say anything but looked intently on as though they understood. Jacky rose and straightened his shirt before he stepped out into the clearing.

The man who had been closest had dragged the bush pole over to the other man and they were both focused on inserting that pole, into a slot on the post by hand. They did not notice the party of three men approach them until they were a few yards away and the first man to look up visibly jumped and in turn startled his mate. "What do you blokes want?" The first man said, letting go of the pole, and standing up straight. He had nothing in his hands, their long axes were on the ground but not in reach. His eyes flickered towards the bush hut and back on Jacky. He looked at the men and assured himself it was safe, as at least two of the savages were wearing normal clothes. The other man who had been straddling the pole, let it drop to the ground and took a step up to be beside the first.

They were both young men, but big, and in their bush jackets and wide hats looked fairly imposing. "Were you sent here by Gellibrand to do this work?" asked Jacky, in a level voice. His brother and Tanapia walked up to be beside him now, Tanapia particularly looking from each man and to the hut.

"Nah mate. We don't work for Gellibrand," the first man

stated, with some air of authority, he noted that while the half-naked savage looked a bit wild these three were unarmed and probably just passing by.

"Well, this is the land of Mr Gellibrand." Jacky retorted as he put his hands on his hips and looked up into the man's face. "All this land along the river is, and out that way too he said, nodding to the west with his head."

"This ain't nobody's land." The first man responded, with a slight grin on his face at the nerve of this black fella. He spat to the side without taking his eyes from Jacky's, the man to his left took a shuffling step forward in support. "And if you think the association land lots still stand, if you understand what that even means, they don't. The land don't belong to no one until they make it their own." The man's voice had raised now, and he seemed to extend himself to his full height and stared Jacky down with his eyes. "And if whoever's fillin' your head with this shit wants to know, my name is Franks, and I'll be managin' this run for Mr Smith as soon as the yards are done and the sheep droved in 'ere."

"Does that mean they are leaving, or not?" Tanapia whispered into Jacky's ear. As he could not understand the language, but he was aware that there appeared to be a stand-off.

Jacky turned right slightly at the sound of the man's voice and answered "No", and in that split second of a distraction, Jacky felt Tanapia's hand on his left shoulder, Tanapia pulled down with his left hand as his right hand came up in full round arc. The new steel axe flashed in the light as the blade caught the man right under his left ear. The axe head buried to more than half its depth and for a moment, the force of the upward

65

blow held the man standing looking down at them with bulging eyes, but as he fell forward Tanapia pulled the axe free and arterial blood sprayed from the cleaved wound that looked as though it was not that far from removing the man's head entirely. Jacky and his brother instinctively jumped back to avoid the spurting blood. The second man had turned to run. Like a horse kicked up to run from a standing start, the man crouched as he turned to get full purchase with his boots in the soil and to propel himself at speed from this aggressor. But as he tried to spring to safety, Tanapia swung the axe again, in a wide overhead arc this time, and brought the axe down so hard that when it struck the man fair in the middle back of his head, it popped like a melon and the man fell sprawling and was dead before he hit the ground. His head was a mess of blood, clear fluid and general gore with his black hair matted in the whole affair.

The second man's hat rolled off his head as he hit the ground and lay a few feet from the dead man's body. Tanapia strolled forward, picked it up and put in on his head. It had a gash in it the square shape of the axe head that matched the hole in the man's head. "That is what you do with men who are not welcome on your land my brother!" He announced proudly. He pulled down the brim of the hat to adjust it to his head and walked on to the makeshift hut.

****

As Tanapia gathered his possessions, the spears he brought with him, his new axe and some food and goods he had plundered from the white man's bush hut, the people of the river camp gathered to watch. Jacky stood over him as Tanapia knelt on the ground putting the goods into one of the large sacks he had stolen. It was clear from Jacky's demeanour that he was watching and waiting, to be sure the man left the camp as soon as possible.

Tanapia stood up, he slung the sack over his shoulder and held the spears upright in one hand. "Take care of yourself and your people" he said in a loud even voice to Jacky, "Do not forget who you are". Tanapia stood up straight and slowly his eyes moved around to meet those of each of the people watching, who stood in a half circle behind Jacky. Men women and children of the camp all silently observing the visitor preparing to leave their lives again forever. As his eyes swept around the row of people, his eyes paused momentarily on the eyes of Jacky's wife and he winked. She inhaled quickly, and almost imperceptibly, and looked at the ground in front of her feet with a frown across her brow. No one else noticed but the foreigner grinned slightly to himself as he turned and walked away.

He headed north-west along the river bank, to find a sheltered place to camp on his own for the night. In the morning he would head out west again across the open plains to get in a whole day of walking so as to get himself back close to his own lands by the following night.

As Tanapia disappeared into the bush and out of their lives Jacky turned to his wife who was still frowning and looking at the ground. He went to her and put his arm around her pulling her head to his chest. "Don't worry about what has happened over the river today" he whispered to her, as the other people from the camp returned to what they were doing and went back to their usual conversations. "I will go and get a message to Gellibrand and he will make it right. It is a good thing that we are a friend of the white man and we can talk with them about what has happened." She looked up into Jacky's face, gave a half-hearted smile as they both turned and headed back to the main camp fire.

Chapter six

A young man, his wild eyes the size of saucers, came cantering into the camp-town on the large horse that he had left with that morning pulling a wagon. "Mr Smith.... Mr Smith..." he was calling. The boy was obviously a good horseman as he held his hat with one hand, the reigns with the other and clung on with his legs to the bareback of the large steed as he steered in into the main road of the camp. He swung down off the horse in the same movement he pulled it up and landed before the port pier. Men from all around were wondering forward to see what the commotion was about. Someone was calling out near the pier and then Mr Smith appeared from a large hut at the end of the row.

"What is all this about lad?" Smith asked as he and another man walked up and looked about to see what was going on. All that he observed, other than men gathering about, was the large snorting horse with frothy white sweat foaming where the boy's knees had evidently rubbed on its sides. The boy stood with his hat tilted right back, panting also himself, looking still wide eyed at the approaching gentleman. "The bush camp sir" the boy gushed "Mr Franks sir..." he stammered on "blood everywhere sir.."

"Calm down boy and explain what is going on. Aren't you Armitage's boy? Where is Franks, and where is the wagon load of supplies you and the other lad left with?" Smith inquired as he bent forward to give his full attention to the clearly frantic young man.

"Yes, my name is Tom Armitage sir. The wagon is fine sir, don't worry about that, it is Mr Franks... and the other man. They're both dead Mr Smith. Both 'ad their 'eads smashed they have!" The boy looked around, and now all the men were leaning in silently, shocked and waiting to hear more of what had happened. All that Tom could hear was the horse blowing air right behind him. Smith met the young man's eyes, raised his eyebrows in surprise and was clearly waiting for a further explanation. "When we got to the bush camp to take the stuff to the blokes workin' out there buildin' the new sheep yards, like you told me. I found 'em both lyin' on the ground where they was workin'. Layin' in puddles of blood they is sir."

"Had they been shot, speared, clubbed? What lad, what did they look like?" Smith asked, the men around him had begun to move uneasily and to talk feverishly amongst themselves with theories of what must have happened. "Shut up you men" Smith snapped as he glared about, "Let young Armitage tell us what he saw."

"Well sir" the young man went on after gathering some confidence, with Smith granting him full attention "They both had one big gash each. One in the side of 'is neck, the other in the back o' the 'ead. The one in the neck was nice and clean like. As if he were hit with a sharp axe. The other a bit hard to tell 'cos 'is head is all smashed like." The boy looked around at Smith and the other men. Many looked at him and then each other, there was a great deal of beard and head scratching going on. "Oh and sir, it had not long ago happened."

"How do you know that lad, what did you see?" Smith inquired, this further information arousing his interest again.

"Well, it was like when we slaughter a lamb" the boy went on "The smell of the fresh blood that was still wet in puddles on the ground.. and I touched Mr Franks, and he is still warm sir. But we didn't see no one about, on the way up or back. No tracks or nothin' either, but someone had messed up the hut pinchin' stuff"

"Hail Mary Mother of....." Smith exhaled softly as he stood up and considered all this. He looked at the young man, "Well done son, you have done well to get back and warn us so quickly." Smith turned to the man he had walked up with "Those black bastards!" he declared though gritted teeth "They are using the same axes we give to them, to kill our own men!" He stormed back toward the large hut from which he came, and his companion scurried to catch up. "Gather up men!" He shouted to no one in particular, and without looking back "We ride out immediately."

****

Buckley, along with most of the roughly 200 people who made up the settlement had heard about the commotion. "We need a couple of the local blacks" he overheard a young bloke calling as he inquired of men he passed as he hurried around between the huts and tents. "Ones who can track and find the black murderers" he called out to anyone who would listen.

"Oh Christ!" Buckley murmured as he grabbed his hat and hustled away back up the hill, away from the port camp. He made his way to one of the more substantial huts near the home of Mr Batman. He found the resident of that hut already standing at the threshold, watching down the hill at the gathering crowd. "Reverend" he called out as he approached, he continued to talk before the other could respond. "You have to 'elp me." The reverend looked at Buckley with melancholy eyes. "They are getting' a mob up... there's gunna be more killins there is..."

"I hear that Mr Franks and his shepherd were killed today" the reverend said calmly, as he continued to watch the goings on. "He was a well-liked and respected man. It will not take much for a frenzy of revenge to take hold of these men. There are no law-makers here to deal with it otherwise William." He turned slowly to look at Buckley's astonished face.

"But I know the blacks better 'n any man" Buckley pleaded. "I know that huntin' them down might end up in a big war. But those men, like Smith and his like, won't listen to me. I'm not good at talkin' with the likes o' them, but you are Reverend, they'll listen to you." Buckley crushed his hat between his hands as he searched the face of the reverend for a sign of compassion.

"Come on then," the Reverend said as he walked off towards the camp. "You can tell me what you reckon I should say on the way."

Smith was on his horse which was whirling and stomping its feet with anticipation. He had his hat and long riding coat on, his saddlebags packed for the possibility of an extended expedition and a blanket roll behind him. "Come on men, we have to get to the Exe River before dark if we are to pick up the tracks of these treacherous bastards! You all knew those good men. You don't want the black cunts getting away do you?"

Around Smith, several other white men were mounting their horses. They each had rifles in their saddle holsters and pistols in their belts. Two of the native men from Sydney were also on horse-back and sitting calmly, ready to ride. A trio of the local natives had been dispatched to run ahead as soon as they had been recruited and briefed on the situation.

From what Smith had been told though, the use of trackers was just a formality. It was well known that the gentleman who had originally claimed section 12 of the Association land, one Mr J.T. Gellibrand, had been petitioning the support of the local tribe. Despite being currently located in Hobart, it was Gellibrand who was really behind all these troubles in the mind of Smith and his crew. Gellibrand had kept warning drovers not to stop on the Exe River but to go and make camp further to the south west. He had told the natives to keep the shepherds off his land even after he was told that the Association claims were rejected by the Colonial powers and therefore non-existent. And now the consequences of that deal with these black savages had come to fruition. All Smith and his men really had to do was find the camp of that mob that lived on the river, which would not be difficult at all, but he had to keep the vehemence of the men up, in case their

73

temper cooled and they failed to follow through with the retribution. Gellibrand's co-conspirators would learn not to fuck with the likes of Mr Smith and his men.

As Smith wheeled his large brown gelding around to set out and lead this campaign, he was confronted by the imposing mass of William Buckley and the local reverend standing in his path. He held his horse back and looked from one to the other with some dismay. "What exactly, are you intending to do here Mr Smith?" The Reverend inquired, with his arms folded, and clearly not intending to move out of the path of the party of riders. Buckley stood beside the Reverend, his hands on his hips, looking up at Smith with a pained expression.

"Move out of the way Reverend" Smith said, in his most carefully controlled tone. "This needs to be done and needs to be done now!" His horse stomped at the ground, plainly as keen as his master to get moving. Smith glared down menacingly at the pair who stood in his way. "The blacks who have gone ahead have already told us that this tribe from over the river are the most dreaded and murderous bastards on the whole mainland."

"You well know, gentleman," the Reverend stated as he looked about the group of men on the horses, each with their eyes fixed firmly on his, "that you have no way of knowing who has offended against us in this most horrendous way. And the local blacks, like most of the native tribes in any area, are always at war with their neighbouring tribes, so of course they will say that they are the murderous ones."

"Yes Reverend, but if we wait it will be only harder to know who did it. Wont it? And we have no magistrate here.

Do we?" Smith challenged the reverend while glaring into his eyes from on top of his large horse. "And what if the savages come in here, and start chopping people's heads off with axes? Aye? What then Reverend?"

"And you Buckley," Smith spat, with clear contempt expressed across his ragged face "I heard you say you would rather go back to live with these black bastards than here in civilisation!"

Smith only had to let his reigns release slightly and his horse jumped forward, on the toe and ready to gallop on, the reverend and Buckley stepped quickly aside. The Reverend rose his fist above his head as the mounted men filed by and bellowed as loudly as he could, in his most authoritarian voice: "Vengeance belongs not to us!"

Buckley stood with his head bent forward looking at the ground as the sound of hooves became distant and the dust drifted off on the soft breeze. "I *would* rather go back to live with the tribe, if this is what he calls civilisation," he said softly, but to no one, as the reverend was already walking back toward his house, shaking his head and still muttering to himself.

****

As dusk fast approached Jacky and the male elders of the river camp held council around the main fire. They discussed with palpable concern the events of the day and the implications for further trouble to follow. There were thoughts of moving to a camp further inland, however drovers with flocks of sheep that had recently passed by to the north, may already be invading those areas. One man suggested that they do what they always did and defend their land from invaders as they had nothing to do with the killings and no one was entitled to move them on from their own lands.

Jacky remained of the view that the relationship that they had built with the leaders of the white men would hold them above blame for the killings. "Stay calm my brothers," he proclaimed, as he looked around the faces of the men in the growing firelight, "I have said that I will go and speak with the leaders of the white men, and I will. I will get a message to Gellibrand and I am sure that he will return to the port camp soon to honour his agreement with us."

The other men looked at the fire or at their feet as they sat in silence contemplating the uncertain future that dogged them in these days of such upheaval and turmoil. They did not challenge Jacky on his point as his tone made it clear that he had made up his mind and it seemed to make sense to all that he should be given the chance at diplomacy, before the mob is forced into running away, or fighting back.

The sharp jangle of metal-on-metal caught their attention and in unison the men all turned to see in the middle distance the bridled head of a brown horse shaking, like a wet dingo, between the trunks of the gum trees. The horse snorted through large round nostrils and held its head high looking straight at the circle of men with the firelight sparkling back from its eyes. The shadows of the bush made it difficult to make out but two younger men, hanging around at the edge of the camp fire saw them first. There was a man squatting at each shoulder of the horse spying on the council of men from the veil of the undergrowth. Two men each in the clothes of white men, but their faces almost completely dark under the wide brims of their hats.

The two young men of the camp, sprung swiftly to their feet and as they had been trained to do, took up a defensive stance between the camp and the unwanted scrutineers. They stood with their feet at more than shoulder with apart, side on, and with a spear half-cocked in their respective throwing arms. Side-by-side they stood glaring straight into the faces of the white men, not thirty yards away peering back from eyes unseen. There was an audible 'click' of two hammers being cocked almost simultaneously as the two interlopers slowly stood up revealing the long arms that they each had held low to the ground, before this confrontation.

The two men stood for a moment with the guns at waist height, pointing in the general direction of the two defenders of the camp. The two boys visibly tensed their arms ready to let loose the spears at any further intimidation. One boy stomped his front foot and grunted in a menacing gesture with the whites of his eyes appearing unnaturally large in the darkness of his face. The men around the circle watched on in silence at the stand-off, which lasted but a few very long seconds. As the young men stood their ground, the shadowy faces of the men faded into obscurity as they stepped backwards until each completely disappeared from view. The horse then turned its hooves and, apparently led by one the reconnoitres, also vanished into the darkness with a flick of a long black tail.

Smith sat on a log by the fire, looking at the partially built sheep yards that were to be the vanguard for the new Mt Cottrell run. A run that he had been envisioning and planning for some months now. A few other men had begun pulling up logs or blankets to sit on also, having tethered their horses for the night. Smith gnawed at a chunk of bread that he had pulled from his saddlebags, and within that wrapped a piece of salted beef.

He turned to look as the sound of horse hooves and tack arose from the banks of the river and the stand of river red gums. A young white man leading his horse and accompanied by a black tracker emerged from the bush to the west. As they approached Smith asked if they had found the savages. "Yeah," the young man replied as he stopped by the fire, his horse nuzzling at his back. "They are not much more than a mile upstream and on the other side. There is a whole camp there, just on the bank of the river, and down along a sand bar."

"How many men?" Smith asked, squinting up at the young man's face lit now only by the glow of the fire.

"Hard to say," he answered, as he pushed his hat back so he could scratch his head in contemplation, "they are a bit on-the-toe you see. They had a couple of warrior types ready with spears. Like guarding the camp I 'spose you'd say. And that ain't all." He added, waited for the attention of the men around the fire, before he added: "Two of those old coons sitting by the camp fire, was wearing straw hats! And I'll bet that they are the very hats taken from the heads of the dead men!" He added, and was greeted with looks of disgust and hate, as he had anticipated.

"Well men," Smith chimed in, "they're armed and ready, so clearly we have found the right camp of the guilty savages. Even apparently sporting the spoils of their crimes with no shame at all!" The men around the fire murmured to each other their abhorrence of the situation now described. "So we will have to ride in fully primed and ready for resistance. Apart from spears it is highly likely they have taken the arms and ammunition from the hut that was plundered here today. There is no reason not to believe that at least a couple of this lot have learnt how to fire a gun so we must act swiftly. He looked around the men who sat by the fire and then slowly back to the young man who still stood waiting with his horse. "Tend to your horse Robbie and then you can draw us a mud-map of the blacks' camp. We can then work out our plan. We will surround the camp at daybreak."

****

Jacky had to extricate himself gently from is wife's embrace as he slipped out of bed. He placed her arm back by her side and pulled the possum skin rug up close around her neck. She stirred slightly but did not open her eyes, not as far as he could tell in the dark anyway, as he quietly left the hut.

He stood outside in the cold still air pissing as he looked across the river to the east. He had been woken by the sound of the warble of a lone magpie that he had taken to mean that it was daybreak. But what he saw on the horizon was barley a distinguishable glow between the silhouette of the bush below and the black sky above. Still speckled with stars high above his head.

With his own rug still wrapped around him, he poked out one arm as he bent down and put a few sticks into the smouldering ash of the main camp fire. He felt with his hand along the grey sandy earth until he turned up a handful of dry gum leaves. These he dropped into the middle of the area of ash where he could feel the most heat still radiating against the sensitive skin of his wrist. He plonked down to sit beside the fire place. Mesmerised by the little sparkling red glows that danced along the thin edges of the long dry leaves, looking for purchase in a crack or tear so as to burst forth into life as an actual flame. As the leaves crackled and curled in the heat, the plume of white smoke filled the air with the smell of eucalyptus. Jacky could feel the strong temptation to stay and tend to the fire, to the usual camp life, that did not involve the daily torments and compromises of dealing with the white invaders. The red embers forming on the leaves sucking at the still air yet searching for the first flicker of a flame.

Well, I am awake now, he thought to himself. He may as well get going into the port camp as soon as he could find his way in the pre-dawn glow and see what he could do to avoid trouble over the deaths of the two white men. He gave in to the desperate lust for life of the hot coals. He cascaded another handful of dry leaves onto the smoking pile and with one sharp puff of his breath was instantaneously bathed in the bright light of new flames. He piled a few sticks and twigs on top of the burning leaves to get the fire going and stood up again. He draped his rug over the front of his hut and buttoned up his red shirt and white trousers. He set off through the bush at a slow pace at first, waiting for his eyes to readjust to the dark after looking into the fire.

****

The wind picked up and blew from the north-west as the sun rose. Smith and his party gathered on the riverbank just 150 yards downstream and south of the camp, where it was unlikely that they would be noticed in the stiff breeze. He had told the men to fan out and watch the camp until he gave the signal to mount up, and ride forward.

There was some smoke blowing from the camp, and now and then the fragments of conversations in the native tongue carried to the assailant's ears. The men became anxious and excited at the same time. This was an ambush on human prey, not kangaroos or a flock of wild ducks. But this was a prey that could fight back, a battle, where they might have expected a counter attack, or even an ambush. All these scenarios had run through their minds and helped justify the blood-lust that was building while they waited for enough light to fill the bush and the signal from Smith to advance.

Smith had two of the black trackers squatting beside him as he hid in the bushes. They had been telling him in a whisper last minute details for the best line of attack for him to ride into the camp. He had earlier held a briefing with all the men so that they all knew the layout for the camp and would sweep through in a co-ordinated fashion in the same direction. He had not wanted one of those over-keen young blokes shooting him in the fray.

As the first rays of the sun beamed across through the tall stand of eucalypts, a mass of what must have been hundreds of white sulphur-crested cockatoos also came streaming down between the trees. Unlike many other types of birds that fly in a formation that turns and steers as one, these cockatoos were flying every which-way and the screeching and squawking completely filled the air to the exclusion of all other sounds. The birds swirled down among the trees like leaves picked up in a mini-tornado and the stark white breasts of the birds flashed in the first rays of the sun just a few yards above the heads of the mounted men.

While this mass exhibition was a spectacular sight to behold, Smith decided to take advantage of the noise and chaotic movement of the birds as a boon to their attack. He took off his hat and waved it, first to the men on his right, and then to those on his left. When he replaced his hat, he kicked his horse up and simultaneously the other mounted men all burst forward from the cover of the scrub, one hand on the reigns, and one with a gun or pistol raised and ready to fire. The black-trackers also ran forward following the horsemen.

They too carried pistols, as they had complained to Smith the night before that they could be attacked and killed by the tribesman themselves for leading the party to the camp. Smith had ordered that some of the men with more than one firearm, loan a pistol to each of the local trackers.

As the mounted men charged into the camp, the tribesmen scrambled for their weapons, but in the commotion and noise of the cockatoos they had been caught unaware. The men were not long out of bed and were preparing for the day around the main camp fire, close to the bush from where the main charge emerged. The weapons of each man, consisting of several spears of varying length and purpose, were propped by the entrance of each man's respective hut, along with a waddie and digging sticks. But many of these tribesmen were cut down by the first volley of shots that ripped through the camp as they had scattered in a desperate plight to arm themselves against this surprise attack.

The men fell about with body and gut shot wounds as the white invaders cut them down. This was a particular and premeditated technique. This was a very successful method of attack used in the hunting of kangaroos in Van Diemen's Land and the men had conspired to employ the same technique against this human quarry.

The theory is this: a kangaroo has a very small head and shoulders and guns are single shot and slow to reload. Kangaroos usually graze as a mob but will disperse very quickly when attacked and go in different directions. So if a hunter attempts to shoot and kill each kangaroo with a careful shot to the head or heart, it is likely he will miss and scatter the whole mob off into the bush. The method developed therefore, is for multiple hunters to charge a mob together, fire one shot at the large gut or hips area of each kangaroo as they sweep through on their horses. They can then turn back and easily finish off the animals that have been maimed by a gut-shot or have had a pelvis smashed by the large lead projectile discharged by these crude weapons.

And so it went here at the river camp. Men were cut down like kangaroos. When they were wounded and incapacitated by gunshot, they were battered about the head by clubs, gun-butts or stirrup irons as the horsemen returned for a second sweep of the camp. The black trackers following the charge of the horses were also able to terminate fallen tribesmen with a pistol or waddie as they picked their way around the huts where the horses had not ventured.

The attack on the men had been very swift and effective. As the mounted men came together near the main camp fire at the conclusion of the second sweep of the camp, their attention was drawn in unison to the ramble below the main camp. As usual the women and children of the camp had been below the high river bank on the sandy area between the water and the steep bank proper. Along this strip of sand and reeds, maybe one or two rods in width, the women and children had rapidly filed as they ran to escape the frightful attack.

This time the attacking party needed no signal to advance. Many of the men had slid their long arms back into the saddle holsters and drew pistols from their belts, while others quickly reloaded guns. The men kicked their horses up so they carefully descended the steep and sandy riverbank onto the flat area beside the water's edge. The women and children screamed and sprinted when they saw this advance and they sprinted along the sand bar, acutely aware that they were trapped between the water and the steep bank. To try to climb the bank would make them easy targets for the mounted men, but to try to outrun the horses was also a futile proposition.

As the men were concentrating on laying back, almost on their horses' rumps, to allow the horses to pick a safe foothold in the soft riverbank as they descended toward the river, Murnin slipped quietly from the sandbar and into the same stand of tall reeds where she and Jacky had laid just a couple of nights before. This had been a terrifying option for Murnin to take, but she knew she had to take action other than running in the open and being an easy target to be shot down. As soon as she was in the stand of reeds, she threw herself down on the sand and rolled onto her stomach. She peered back through the reeds in the direction of the attackers. She held her breath and heard the bare-footed stamping of many desperate people sprinting by. She felt sick with shame as the thought flashed through her mind that she hoped none of her companions would follow her lead and thereby betray her hiding place.

While Murnin laid in the reeds, wracked with absolute terror, she was able to just make out the flicker of riders speeding by, very close to her position. Shortly after she also saw the dark shadows of three or four men on foot run by. She let out a long slow breath and put her face in her hands. Like the goanna that runs to the nearest tree and then lays completely flat and camouflaged against the bark is much more likely to escape, by doing nothing more than staying still, than the lizard that runs across the ground in the open, she had stayed where she lay until these despicable men were all gone. However, Murnin knew even then that she would be forever haunted by the sounds of her sisters, nieces and nephews being slaughtered like wild dogs. The huts were scattered and burnt. And close by she had heard the incomprehensible sound of bodies being dragged and then dumped into the river.

****

Mary waited a long time. Laying with her face down in the sand she had barely moved a muscle until the sounds of the bush had long returned and no trace of the white invaders could be detected. The sun was high and it may have been close to noon by the time she rose to her knees, and peered out from the stand of tall river reeds. Not only was Murnin terrified of being sighted by the murdering band of invading men, she was terrified of the sights that she would find of her family and friends.

To avoid both, she slipped quickly up the riverbank and back into the scattered river red gums that dotted the river flats all along this stretch. She knew exactly where to go, and she knew that place was also where Jacky and anyone else who survived the massacre would go. To the north, about half a day's walk, the river flat reduces to a narrow ravine. Further still that ravine becomes a narrow gorge between steep cliffs and tall mountains. Within that ravine is the most remote and isolated camp that the tribe has on the most northern extreme of their country. It is almost an island in the river formed where the river sweeps around in a horseshoe shape leaving a flat grassy circle of land in the middle, with a near vertical cliff face forming the outer side of the river circle. The bush on the mountains and in the ravine is thick, and inhabited only by the animals adapted to those lands such as wombats and the almost black bush wallaby.

To precipitate her escape and avoid the long meandering course of the river Murnin moved a couple of hundred yards west of the river and followed the tree line north. She could already see the outline of the ranges to the north and set a course to intersect with the river again in a couple of hours. She hoped that she might then find the tracks of other survivors who had also followed the river north, but she tried not to think about who might be dead or alive, as she would become racked with guilt at the very thought of her own actions in hiding back there by the river alone.

Murnin walked on, only focusing on the distant ranges and getting to safety, when suddenly as she passed a large wattle bush she was grabbed and dragged back under the canopy of the scrub. There was a strong arm across her chest and a hand on her mouth when he dragged her down to sit with her back against his chest. She struggled and tried to turn to see who had hold of her, but she was somewhat relieved that at least the skin of the arm that restrained her was black. A man's deep voice said quietly to her "It is alright, I just didn't want you to scream if I startled you..." he relaxed his grip and slowly took his hand off her mouth "... I heard the guns and men on horses, I was coming back to see what happened."

Slowly Murnin sat forward and put her face in her hands and wept. She did not turn to face him, she knew that it was Tanapia. After a minute or two she replied "They charged into the camp before anyone was ready, it was barely daylight.

The men were killed before they could even start to fight back. They put holes in everyone that they saw. And with their horses, they ran down and clubbed everybody else, even the little children." She glanced at Tanapia for a moment with tears welling up again in her eyes, she put her head in her hands and continued to sob.

After hearing this Tanapia stood up, still within the cover of the scrub, and peered back towards the main camp. "So, all the men are dead." He said, in a tone that suggested he was pondering this situation, rather than asking a question of her. "No!" she retorted sharply "Jacky had left before daylight, to go to the port camp." She looked Tanapia squarely in the eyes and gained a sudden conviction about this "He would have heard the guns too, he will also be on his way north to the gorge camp and is probably coming along this way now." She looked around, as if Jacky may appear right on cue.

"What ever happened we have to get away quickly" Tanapia said sternly as he pulled Murnin to her feet by the wrist. "Those white men will cut us down just as quickly too if they see us from their horse's backs." He led her along at a fast walking pace through the trees, still pulling her along with his strong grip on her wrist, his spears held in a bunch upright in is other hand. She was content to be led away for a while, as she was just relieved to have someone else living with whom to escape. However, after a while she looked around. They were leaving the trees of the river flat and walking onto the open grassy plains. Murnin then said to her pilot "You are going too far west, we have to go more north to reach the gorge camp." As she looked over her right shoulder at the ranges in the distance, to indicate the way they should be headed.

"We are not going to this gorge camp," he said and his grip on her wrist tightened as he pressed on and pulled Murnin along with him, not turning to face her at all. "We are going home!"

****

Jacky was quite a way down the river when he heard the echo of the distant gunshots. He felt goose bumps all over his body as a chill ran deep to his heart. He had been picking his way through a eucalypt forest and he then turned back upstream. He wanted to run home, but his legs had turned to jelly and he slumped back against a tree. He put his head back and looked at the blue sky and he heard the multiple gunshot continuing and while he didn't want to think about it, he knew exactly what was happening. The white men were taking wrongful revenge against his people, and there he was standing there alone, helpless.

It had taken Jacky well over an hour to get back to the camp. As he approached the camp and there was no sign of life, he felt as though a hand had reached in and ripped out his stomach, so horrendously ill it made him feel. He walked through the camp and all he saw was blood splatters and the marks on the sand where bodies had been dragged away. He hurried now down to the river, where many bodies floated in the water and others were snagged in the reeds. He scanned the female bodies for the face of his wife. He did not react to the sight of his dead countrymen and women. He had to shut emotions out as best he could and focus on trying to find survivors. He had seen the little footprints of where children had run up-river along the sandy track, and while he continued to look at the bodies as he went, he also followed those tracks.

When Jacky could not see his wife among the bodies in the river, he continued to follow the river upstream. They had a camp in the north that everyone knew to go to if there was a disaster on their land or they became lost or separated. He did not need to follow the footprints to see if there were any survivors, he already knew exactly where they would be going.

It was getting dark that evening when Jacky was nearing the mouth of the gorge where the northern gorge camp was located. Large pools of water formed at this flat area of land where the river spilled from the narrow gorge and became calm between clean deposits of sand and fine river gravel washed over thousands of years down the valley, and further carving out the steep gorge. He sat down cross-legged at the edge of the water and drank from his hand the cool clean mountain water.

He looked at the mouth of the gorge, with a very steep bank to the left sloping down from a high mountain peak behind which the sun was now hiding. The right bank was guarded by a sheer cliff that the setting sun made appear a deep orange animated by the many fairy martins that dived and darted about in front of the rocky cliff face.

The birds made Jacky aware that he was in a different place. A safe place. He had left behind the open plane and was enveloped in the safety of the ranges. Many small woodland birds were hopping about in the thick foliage above his head, silhouetted against the sky. A flock of crimson rosellas squawked in warning to other bush animals when it flew out of the gorge and had been collectively surprised by the presence of the man sitting by the water.

Jacky lit no fire to betray his whereabouts that night and he had no appetite for food in any case. He lay down on the soft sand bank below the cliff face and watched the black bush wallabies creep down to the water to drink in the last of the light before he fell asleep.

In the morning light Jacky drank from the stream and washed the night from his eyes. He swept the sand bank smooth from his footprints as he walked backwards onto the rocks at the base of the cliffs. He hopped from rock to rock along the base of the cliff until he reached a low bank covered in ferns, other than where wombats had carved out their large burrows and made tracks along the river bank when they went foraging in the night. He walked easily on the grey sandy tracks and followed the meandering river north for about two miles up the narrow gorge. It was cool and moist in the ferns and tea-tree undergrowth, overshadowed by very tall and straight mountain gum trees, with impressive hard and smooth white trunks.

Eventually he came to the place where the river turned almost back on itself, forming a round and flat area of land with a green grassy cover, and this area contained a large ring of coals from camp fires many months and years previous. He immediately sat down on the soft grass beside the fire place facing across to a very large deep pool of water, with a sheer cliff-face backing. He pictured in his mind memories of himself as a boy, with his friends and siblings, jumping from a ledge on that cliff into the pool of water below. One of the few places along this river where it was deep enough to do this safely.

While he sat there reminiscing, he wondered if the children would ever experience the freedom that he had as a child. He absent-mindedly snapped small twigs and gathered dry leaves that were within easy reach of where he sat. He made a pile of kindling ready to start a fire later in the day when he would gather some more substantial firewood. Jacky did not need to search the area to see who else had made it to the camp, he had already known from the signs that small feet had scampered up the river tracks ahead of him.

The children had stayed huddled behind a fallen log a couple of chain up the hill, and upriver from the camp-site, as they had been taught to do. All wide eyes turned to the eldest boy, to sneak down and see who was making the noise snapping twigs, and if it was safe for them to come out of the bush.

Chapter seven

A large gathering of people turned out for the funeral of Mr Franks and his shepherd. The graves had been dug on the hill above the Yarra River, where the flagstaff that signalled to the ships in port was set. The cold wind was strong up on the exposed hillside and matched the sombre mood of the mourners. It was a big shock to these pioneers to realise that to settle in these lawless lands was a risk to anyone among them of suffering the same fate as that which befell poor Mr Franks.

William Buckley had been very much disturbed by the events of the previous couple of days. He had come into the white man's settlement with the very intention of avoiding a war between the settlers and the native population. Now the people who had cared for him and allowed him to live as a part of their extended family for 30 years were being slaughtered for defending their own lands, by money hungry invaders. He could not bring himself to join the funeral party, as the Reverend gave his sermon at the graveside, but he hovered at the edge of the camp, muttering to himself about how he had said that this would happen, but no one had listened to him. One of the men, Sutherland, who was standing at the back of the crowd, could hear Buckley muttering under his breath. He called between gritted teeth "Why don't you fuck off back to the blacks you disrespectful cunt".

Buckley walked back to his own hut immediately and began to pack up his few belongings. On that day he had determined that he could not bear to be a part of this settlement any longer. He was no longer a part of the native community, and as it turned out, he could not fit back into the English community either.

That night at the port town, some of the men who had taken part in the raid on the Exe River camp sat around a fire drinking. They were recounting the raid to other men of the camp who sat around drinking as well, all staring into the fire, as though the event were being acted out by players dancing in the flames. There was a mixture of emotions among the men of the raid that night. Some were downcast and introspective, keeping quiet and dousing their apprehensions with rum. Others were more boastful about the deeds that had been committed that morning, as though they had been celebrating a brave battle that had been fought and won.

Mr Smith approached the fire and happened upon the scene just as a young man named Cowley was boasting about the number of blacks that he and the other mounted men had slain. "We fucken' annihilated them black animals" he slurred, as he paused for effect, and to take another swig of rum, "We knocked down every black bastard before they knew what 'it 'em... ha ha ha..." he trailed off. The other men around the fire shuffled uncomfortably at this and gave young Cowley only sideways glances. Mr Smith took him from behind by the upper arm and lifted Cowley to his feet, "Come here you drunken fool, you don't know what you're talking about." He whispered, but loudly enough for all the men around the fire to hear. As he led Cowley away, he pointed out the other men from the raid who were present. "You, you and you, come over here as well."

"Don't you fools know that the Gov'nor in Sydney Town, will hang you as quick for a black man as any other man?" Smith barked in a hushed, but severe voice as he looked the young men each in the eyes as they gathered in a circle around him, far enough from the camp fire not to be overheard. "We talked about this today didn't we?" He looked pleadingly around the faces for some semblance of intelligence.

"Yeah," one of Cowley's mates piped up "We fired shots into the black's camp to scare 'em off. We don't think anyone got shot but we drove them off to keep the settlers safe. Oh, and the blacks had stolen guns and they fired at us too." The young man looked to Mr Smith, pleased with himself for having remembered the story correctly.

"That's right McGinty", Mr Smith affirmed, "We fired shots, scared the blacks off, and that is all we are saying, right." He glared at Cowley with another fierce look, "Or it will be you young Cowley that will hang from the noose, and not me, if you keep spoutin' off shit like that. Now fuck off out'a my sight before I do you in myself." The young men scurried off about the camp, eager to get away from the scorn of Mr Smith.

However, news of the boasting about the massacre at the Exe River had spread like wildfire throughout the port town. One settler in particular named Mr Beecroft had heard the claims by young Cowley and had been most upset by the revelations that innocent people had been slaughtered in the name of bush justice. He could not reconcile in his mind how the murder of two white shepherds could possibly justify the killing of a whole tribe of the local people. How could a whole tribe be guilty of the crimes of just one or two individuals?

Beecroft sat down at a desk in his small hut and set out a candle, inkwell and paper. He took up a pen and drafted two heartfelt letters that night. One to the Governor of Van Diemens Land, from whence Beecroft had originally journeyed, and one to Mr JT Gellibrand with whom he had had a previous encounter at this port town.

****

Gellibrand was furious when he read the letter from Beecroft a couple of weeks after the incidents at Mt Cottrell had occurred. He stomped around in the office of his home in Hobart while his, by that time, adult son Thomas sat at a chair by the desk watching and listening with concern to his father. Joseph T Gellibrand read the letter out loud to his son as he paced about in the sunlight coming in through the window.

"He is asserting that we have employed natives to drive the settlers off the land we claimed through our treaty with the natives!" JT Gellibrand stated as he stopped pacing but continued to gaze at the page in his hand. "And it is possible that the Death of Mr Franks may be thus imputed." He let his hands and the letter fall by his side, he then turned to look at young Thomas Gellibrand "This Mr Beecroft is telling people that we are paying the blacks to guard our land with lethal force, and that the deaths that have recently come about are somehow connected with us and our relationship with the local tribe on our lands. This is an outrage!" JT Gellibrand cried, with his voice rising as his anger also appeared to rise.

Thomas asked him in a mild voice "What are we to do about this father?" Thomas knew that his father would not long be held by emotions but would soon turn to practical solutions as he had seen so many times. As a very good lawyer and barrister his father had often confronted complex problems, explored options, and then found a resolution. JT Gellibrand had been well practised at putting aside emotional investment and sentimentality to confine an issue to the facts of the matter and quantifiable outcomes.

"First," JT Gellibrand went on, "I will write to the Governor setting out that I deny most vigorously any and all accusations by Beecroft that our actions were somehow tied to the death of Franks and his shepherd. In fact, I will tell Governor Bourke, that I had pressed Franks personally to run his flock somewhere within Selection 12 for the next six months, but not to settle on the Exe River area." JT Gellibrand stood by the window looking up into the sky as though composing the letter in his mind. Thomas looked up at him, waiting for him to continue with the plan. "Also, I will meet with my connections in the local press and make sure that they do not run any stories on the murders in Port Philip that repeat these accusations. And then Tom, we must make haste with our plans to return to Port Philip. We will take over more stock and supplies for our selection. We will also continue our exploration of the area to the west so we will go in the summer when we can ford the rivers that we saw last time."

J T Gellibrand resumed his pacing and looked to the floor. Thomas could see that his father's usual calm and driven demeanour had returned as he had devised his plans for another Port Phillip expedition. "Tom, you can help out. Round up all the gentlemen who are interested in coming on the next expedition and arrange a meeting one night in the next couple of weeks at The Club. Oh, and invite Mr Hesse, we were talking the other day in chambers and he is interested in investing in Port Phillip as well. Then find a brig that will be sailing to Port Phillip early in the New Year."

Chapter eight

*T*he *Henry* sailed up the bay at a slow rate, given the warm north-westerly that was blowing that morning in February 1837. JT Gellibrand spoke with the captain of the vessel, Captain Treguntha, in his cabin about negotiating a return trip in about 2 weeks' time. Captain EP Treguntha had transported around 10,000 head of sheep between Van Diemens Land and the mainland in recent years and had even encouraged his own sister and brother-in-law to seek to set up their own sheep run on the mainland. The Captain said "Well you may be in luck Mr Gellibrand. We usually have about a 7 to 10 day stop in port before we depart again for Launceston. But, on this occasion we have been chartered to make 5 runs between Williamstown and Corio Bay. For the new sheep runs around the new settlement between Corio Bay and Indented Heads, the company that owns them has discovered it is quicker and easier to move stock and supplies by ship than over the land. It will not be long before there is a busy port built on Corio Bay as well, and then we'll be sailing straight from Lonny to the new port instead of Williamstown. I understand that you and the other gent's want to ride from Corio Bay to Williamstown to inspect your properties?" Gellibrand, who had been admiring the shipping charts spread out on the desk that the Captain had himself created of the entrance to Port Phillip, looked up and nodded. "Well, with respect Mr Gellibrand, it only takes a couple of days to ride around the bay. Even if you spent a couple of days on your property, that don't take two weeks?"

"Yes, you are correct Captain. But we also want to go west first and visit a couple of the other runs that some other chaps have set up along the river there. Two of your other passengers that we have met on board, a Mr Cowie and a Mr Stead, have kindly offered to let us stay at their camp tonight at a place called the Duck Holes and we will head west from that camp tomorrow."

"Oh, I see'" the Captain replied, not surprised, but then in a voice with a hint of concern "But you blokes know what you are doing don't you? No offence you know, but you don't exactly look like the greatest bushman. 'Specially that young bloke George, that lawyer, he looks like he's never set foot outside of his office." The Captain said with a cheeky grin. He was then quite a bit younger than Gellibrand, but could afford to be a bit cheeky, given his extensive experience and the fact that he co-owned his own shipping line from the wealth he was then generating from the new settlers. "But anyway, I 'spose it is hard to get lost because that little mountain range, that runs along the top end of the bay, you can see that from many, many miles away. You probably know the big one as Station Peak?" He went on, as Gellibrand nodded "And if you always have that range in view, and the bay in view, you just keep the peak on your left, the bay to your right, and you have to end up at Williamstown."

"I think we can manage that." Gellibrand remarked, flashing his own superior grin. "And we did travel these areas about this time last year, with William Buckley as our guide. You know, the one known as the wild white man? He was a useful guide, but thick as a brick when it came to any detailed information about the land."

"But you don't seem to have much in the way of equipment? I see you only stowed a canvas bag each, with your blanket rolls and tack. You do have equipment, don't you? You know, for navigation and all?"

"Ah, as you said, travelling over land we only need to follow the land marks. You know the rivers, the hills, the bay."

"Well anyway," The Captain said, as he opened one of the desk draws to his left and rummaged around for something, "Take this with you," and he then produced what looked like a small silver pocket watch and passed it across to Gellibrand.

Gellibrand turned it in his hand and then laid it flat on his palm to watch the spinning, floating needle of the pocket compass, until it settled pointing north. "Thank you, Captain." He said smiling over the desk at the young man, "I will be sure to give it back on the return voyage."

When Gellibrand stood up to leave, he reached across to shake hands with the Captain. While still holding Gellibrand's hand in his firm grip the Captain stated "Fourteen days Mr Gellibrand. Fourteen days is all I can give you. If you blokes are not at Williamstown by that time I will have to leave, you will soon find another vessel heading back."

****

The Brig had to unload the horses and Gellibrand's party at Point Henry, as the ship could not get so close to shore further around Corio Bay. Captain Treguntha told the party, consisting of Gellibrand, Mr George Brook Legrew Hesse, the young lawyer from Hobart, and a Mr Sinclair, another prospective settler who had been keen to explore the lands further, to ride their horses around the bay until they came to a make-shift port near the mouth of a creek. Another passenger named Roadnight, had also unloaded his horse at Point Henry however he was not part of the explorers' party and was riding to a property towards Williamstown alone. The brig, the captain explained, can sail around to the creek and then unload other passengers who don't have horses and cargo with the use of row boats.

Gellibrand and the other three horsemen rode slowly around to the creek, where they had to wait for the ship to unload the cargo and to get their gear for the expedition to begin. On the way around to the creek, Gellibrand was chatting with Roadnight. Hesse and Sinclair had ridden on ahead as Sinclair's horse had been a bit on-the-toe since being on the ship and needed a run to settle him down. When Gellibrand told Roadnight about his plan to explore the western plains further, Roadnight said to him "Don't be goin' off to the Duck Holes tonight if you blokes are plannin' to go west. The Duck Holes are away up there, up past that swampy area where we passed across the bay." He looked across at Gellibrand with a furrowed brow, "I have been around this area many times and there is a ford in the main river, it is only a couple of miles south west of this makeshift port we are

102

headin' to now. Not even two miles I reckon."

"Yes, that sounds like good advice Mr Roadnight. I would appreciate if you could point us in the right direction, from the creek."

"Hell, I can do better than that, for a fellow country gent," Roadnight said, with a friendly smile and a wink, "I'll ride over with you and make camp for the night myself. I don't care much for the Duck Hole swamp with all its mossies and snakes!" he laughed.

As they rode on, the hillside above the makeshift port came slowly into view. Many camps and some buildings had appeared on the hill since Gellibrand last explored this area which was largely a barren hillside at that time. A wagon track was visible leading up from the muddied water's edge to wind between the settlement of mainly tents and huts. But his attention was drawn quickly back to the waterfront, by some sort of commotion. A group of people were gathering around someone on the ground.

When Gellibrand and Roadnight rode their horses up to the site of the gathered people, they saw that the man lying on the ground was Sinclair. Hesse was kneeling beside him, and clearly Sinclair was in pain. He writhed around holding his leg in both hands. Hesse looked up at the mounted men "He got thrown off his horse.... well" he tried to explain, "He sort of got thrown, but tried to jump off. Anyway, he landed really rough, I think he broke his ankle."

Gellibrand got down off his horse and, with the reins in his hand, bent down to look at the injury. The other people lost interest and went back to their business of collecting goods being unloaded from row-boats. He gently pulled Sinclair's trousers back up the leg and untied the boot. As soon as he pulled the flaps of the boots apart, he could see the ankle was starting to swell. "I'll leave the boot on for now," Gellibrand said to the injured young man, who was by then beginning to compose himself and control the pain, "Because if you take it off, you won't get it back on again in a hurry! But there is no deformity in the bones or from what I can see of the ankle, so I don't think it is broken. By the looks of the swelling though, you got a very bad sprain."

The men helped Sinclair to the grassy bank away from the muddy waterside and they all sat down to rest after tethering the horses. Someone had already got a fire going, probably still there from when someone made lunch, so Mr Roadnight put a billy of water on to make tea. Gellibrand and Hesse contemplated what they would do about Sinclair and his injury.

It was clear to Gellibrand and Hesse that Sinclair would not be able to ride his horse much further, but they wanted to see if the injury improved or got worse before they decided what to do. The men all sat about together on the grassy bank staring at the smoke from the fire, while they sat there sipping at their mugs of billy tea. No one spoke for some time, but eventually, Sinclair blurted out, "I'm sorry Mr Gellibrand, but I won't be able to go on and ride with you gentlemen, on your expedition." He looked across the fire at them, with pleading eyes.

"That's all right son, I can see that you would not be able to ride far in that condition" Gellibrand replied. Sinclair laid back against the grassy bank and massaged his leg above the knee. Gellibrand and Hesse looked at each other, sipping their tea, both had been thinking it was about time that they moved on.

Gellibrand told Hesse how Mr Roadnight had volunteered to take them across to a camp-site near the river. The men all got up and began to pack their goods and to ready their horses for the further ride to the camp-site. It had been arranged that Sinclair would go with the others to the duck holes and from there could be taken back to Williamstown by the other men. And so, Gellibrand and Hesse began their expedition together being led by their guide Mr Roadnight away from the bay up across the hill, where Gellibrand had seen the buildings, that would eventually form the town of Geelong. Nearly at the top of the hill the three men stopped their horses and turned to look back across the bay. There were several ships moored in the harbour, and quite a lot of general activity down at the makeshift port. It was quite an excellent site for a new port town and looking back across the bay the men could see smoke rising from the distant camp town that had become Williamstown.

Mr Roadnight led the two explorers down the Hill into a river valley. There was a substantial river running through the valley and they walked the horses down the path that led to some beautiful natural ponds formed by large boulders blocking parts of the river. Some of these ponds were probably about two chains across at the widest point. Roadnight pointed out that there were already plans to further dam the river at this point as a place to build water-driven mills to support the growing town. They walked the horses for a short time along the bank of the river where there was an expansive river flat and they eventually came to a wagon trail leading to the river where there was a shallow ford.

As they approached the wagon trail that evening, they could see smoke rising from the small camp fire and beyond that near the river bank was a covered dray with several bullocks grazing nearby. Sitting hunched over the fire was a large burly man with the scruffy black beard. As he stoked the coals of the fire, preparing it for cooking, he squinted up through the smoke at the approaching riders and a smile appeared across his face. He pushed his hat back on his head and greeted the men warmly.

The men dismounted and approached the camp fire. The man's name was John Aikers and he explained to the trio that he was a bullock team driver who had recently started working in the area. Although it was hot, the men naturally settled in around the fire and conversed with their new acquaintance. As it turned out to Gellibrand and Hesse, Mr Aikers was a likeable and jovial fellow and they had decided to accept his offer to share this camp-site with him for the evening. Gellibrand, Hesse, Aikers and Roadnight all supped by the quiet river and shared stories of explorations in these lands before going to sleep on their bed rolls for the evening.

In the morning, after a quick billy of tea, Mr Roadnight bid the men farewell and a safe journey as he rode off to the North. Aikers explained to the men that he was taking a wagon loads of goods to Capt. Pollock's station, the same place that Gellibrand and Hesse were scheduled to visit that day. He told them that he had recently made several trips to Capt. Pollock's station as Pollock and another settler in the area were improving their new homesteads and his dray was the only way of getting bulk supplies out there. He told the two men that they could ride ahead and easily follow his wagon trail along the river and that if they stayed on that trail and within sight of the river, they would soon come to the ford and Pollock's Station. Aikers told them that he would be along later in the day, as his dray pulled by bullocks could only make 2 to 3 miles per hour.

It was a warm sunny morning as Gellibrand and Hesse forded the shallow river crossing and made their way west. They followed the tracks left by Aikers bullock dray, easily visible in the long dry grass. They kept the main river to their left which meandered along in a generally west direction with an expansive plane stretching out before them and a steep row of hills on the south side of the river opposite to where they rode.

The two men were struck by how large and expansive this plane was. Gellibrand explained to the younger man how he had heard about this plain and had only seen the edge of it on his last expedition. Unlike the soil on the run he had established in the Exe River area that did not hold moisture in the summer and autumn months but became dry cracked and rocky once the vegetation dried off, the soil on this plane was dark and heavy and kept the cover of grass much better through the hot dry months that was often experienced in is part of the world.

As far as the two men could see in front of them and to the north-west the land stretched out relatively level speckled intermittently with large old gum trees. The native grass came up halfway on the horse's legs and in the early morning there were lots of birds flitting around the trees and the grass and occasionally a pair of black ducks would rise from a pond on the river as they passed by. Not far into their journey as their horses walked slowly along, they put up a small mob of kangaroos that had been resting in the shade of one of the large gum trees. While the kangaroos had initially been startled they only hopped a short distance before they sat up tall and stared back at the unusual creatures with the men on their backs.

As the men sauntered along awestruck by the visions around them, Gellibrand pulled a small glass bottle from his waistcoat and shook from it two white powdery pills. "I can't handle these long hot days and long rides like I could as a young fellow, like you Mr Hesse" Gellibrand mused as he popped two pills into his mouth and took a swig from his canteen. "In fact, I'll have to take a rest mid-morning to recover and lay down before we continue our journey on to Captain Pollock's. We have all day to get there and it is only about 8 or 10 miles away. At least I have a supply of these calomel pills for when I feel this extreme lethargy, and by the way, let me know if you need any."

Hesse smiled and nodded and went back to looking around at all there was to be seen in this seemingly untouched region. George Hesse was a naturally shy young man and also a lawyer. Relatively new to the colony of Van Diemens Land, he had been quite excited about this expedition. He had only just been getting used to the landscape of Van Diemens Land at that time and he had been quite taken by the adventurous nature of this journey into relatively uncharted territories. The settlement of Capt. Pollock's station, the ford and the station of Mr Swanston were then at the extreme western frontier of the whole mainland colony centred on the Yarra Yarra area.

Gellibrand and Hesse

George Hesse felt like a young warrior pushing the boundaries of this wide and brand-new frontier. Although given the high standing and serious nature of his companion, George had tried to contain his enthusiasm.

As the men rode up to a particularly large river red gum above a large pond on the river, Gellibrand suggested that they rest here and make a small fire for a billy of tea. As was often the case, under this large gum were lots of dry twigs, branches and eucalyptus leaves and so young Hesse busied himself gathering up a bundle of these to make a small fire. While he did this, Gellibrand unfastened his belt, loosened his waistcoat and laid down in the shade with his head on his bed roll for a pillow. Hesse let the older man rest while he prepared tea by going down to the river and taking a scoop of water in the small billy.

While squatting beside the water Hesse again became amazed at the extent of the wildlife in this area, with ducks and swans swimming away from his approach down the river, little wrens flitting between the tops of the reeds. He particularly admired the superb blue fairy wren that was only a few feet from him, with its brilliant blue patches around its eyes and black and white plumage. The small brown female wren was very plain by comparison. He noticed that suddenly the small birds seemed to startle and disappear back into the scrub and reeds, and he wondered why they were scared of him, when moments before they seemed oblivious to his presence? This question was answered, when he looked up and was also surprised to see a huge eagle gliding silently through the air maybe only 20 feet above, and following the course of, the river. The wing span of the eagle was as wide as a man is tall. As the huge eagle came over George Hesse it banked slightly and started to circle around quickly gaining altitude on an apparent updraught of air between the plane and the steep hills. It circled around above his head until it was very high in the sky directly above the river.

Later the two men continued their plodding journey in a generally west direction following the wagon trail marks left by previous trips of the bullock dray of Mr Aitkers. They admired the geography of the ancient river course where in places the river had carved out steep escarpments that exposed rocks of orange and brown hues. And in other places meandered peacefully beside flat open fields. Along the way Gellibrand told stories to young Hesse about his experiences as a barrister and lawyer in Van Diemens Land and also of his early days when first admitted to the bar in London. Hesse asked many questions about Gellibrand's stories and was keen to soak up the wealth of knowledge that this older lawyer had acquired in the new colony.

As the men came around a bend in the river, they saw a substantial building on the next rise and a man was already out the front ready to greet them. That man was Captain Pollock, who had claimed this land as his own. Some 18,000 acres in fact. "Gentlemen!" He called loudly as he strode up and shook hands first with Gellibrand and then with the younger man Hesse. "Please come inside and have some lunch, one of the boys will see to your horses." Gellibrand and Hesse dismounted and wrapped the reigns around the hitching posts by the front door of the home. They noticed that the house was positioned on a rise with a bend in the river practically wrapping itself right around the house yard. It certainly was a very pretty position for a home.

While the men ate lunch at a large wooden table in the homestead, Gellibrand and Pollock talked a lot of politics, and particularly about the granting of land in the new colonies. Gellibrand was obviously displeased generally with the way the place was governed and with the allocation of crown land. "The problem" Gellibrand kept pointing out "is that the sloths in the government can't keep up with the progress of its people. Instead of supporting those people who are developing the land, investing funds, and employing the workers; all they do is put up barriers and retard those people." To which Capt. Pollock agreed. Although at the time, Hesse had little interest in such matters and still had his mind turned to thoughts of the many adventures yet to come.

Hesse did prick his ears however when Capt. Pollock told the story of how he was presently without the services his best stock-man. He raised the story in the context of grumbling about the government causing problems, however the chilling tale he told was this: "You see we had this big black bastard, pinching stuff from around the station and I am sure also stealing sheep, although I never did catch him directly. He was a general troublemaker always sneaking around on his own and then heading back to the hills where his people are camped. Well you see, my stockman named Fred Taylor and the couple of the younger boys caught him sneaking around behind the stockyards and they grabbed him and tied him up for the purpose of taking him into the port to have something done about his outlaw activities." Capt. Pollock continued, in a level tone as he continued to eat his mutton casserole and bread. "So they tied him to a tree, with a cord around his wrists behind his back, and a cord around his neck attaching him to the tree. And left one of the boys, young Whitehead, there with a rifle to guard him, and Taylor and the other boy went to find me."

Gellibrand and Hesse listened on intently to Captain Pollock as he continued with his story: "But it all turned to shit, you see, when the black fella started hollering a hideous noise the likes you'd never have heard. He was looking to the sky screaming and hollering like you would not believe. Anyway, this really spooked the young bloke who was left to guard him on his own and he tried to shut the black fella up.

But the black fella just wouldn't stop and when the young bloke saw that he was looking to the Hills he panicked. He thought that this bloke was calling his clan to come down from the hills and Whitehead must have thought that he was certainly at risk of an imminent attack." He looked to Gellibrand and Hesse and paused for dramatic effect.

"So the young bloke is there tryin' to stop this crazy black bloke hollering to his mates and he's got the rifle pointed at the black fella's body. Well, I can't be sure what happened next, but the young fella says that the gun discharged accidentally, shooting this bloke right in the guts at point blank range." Hesse looked with an open mouth astounded at how calmly Captain Pollock relayed this shocking story of such recent events. "Then, because he thought a whole tribe of black fellas were gunna come out of the hills, he rolled the dead body into the water leaving it tethered on the cord." Captain Pollock broke a piece of bread and mopped up the gravy on his plate. "And that gentlemen, is how I found the scene. The young bloke Whitehead sitting on the bank in tears and the body floating in the river with a cord around its neck. And, that is also how I lost my best stockman, because they not only took away the young bloke, but they summoned Mr Taylor as a witness to go all the way to bloody Sydney for the trial. Such a bloody inconvenience! And all the black fellas south-west of here, they call the Karakois, are now apparently on the war path over the death of that one big bastard."

The gentlemen all rested for a while in the house after lunch, and in the late afternoon Captain Pollock showed the men around the yard and down to the ford where a natural rocky run created a shallow crossing point on the river just below the house yard. The steep earth bank leading down from the east and the rocky outcrop on the steep bank opposite made for a very pretty scene. "You two gentlemen let your horses rest, cross the ford, and take a stroll up that big hill" he pointed up to the peak of the largest hill on the opposite side of the bank. "You can see all the land that you're seeking to explore from up there, and it is a spectacular view as the sun goes down in the west."

The two men took the opportunity, and after picking their way across the shallow water, began the ascent zigzagging up the side of the very steep hill. One of the first things they noticed from their elevated position was that Aikers was approaching the home with his bullock team. He was coming across the flat, a couple of hundred yards away from the homestead, walking beside his bullocks with a long stick with the whip at the end urging the large beasts on at a steady pace.

When they reached the top of the hill, they found that they were on the highest peak of this range of hills and that they could see for many miles in every direction. They could see back along the river whence they came, and along the row of hills to the east. To the south, more hilly country, but their interests lay in the land to the west and north-west of their location. From this elevated position, they could see that there was miles and miles and miles of open plane land perfectly suitable for agriculture. Assuming this river continue through the plane there will also be ample water to sustain stock.

"That is where we have to explore, George." Gellibrand said to the young companion. "That is where the best and biggest runs can be established, on those planes out there, just waiting for someone to claim them." George Hesse just looked on in awe at the expanse of the land before them. "We must have a look out there before we return to Williamstown. We may never have an opportunity like this again George." He looked at the young man intently, his own face beaming with excitement.

"Yes Mr Gellibrand, I believe we must." Young Hesse stated and this time the enthusiasm of the adventure was written all over his face. He felt his belly churn and his bowels turning to water at the prospect of the unknown that awaited them in the coming days.

****

That evening, after dinner, Pollock, Gellibrand, Hesse and Aikers sat outside smoking and sharing a bottle of rum. It was very pleasant outside, as the heat of the day had made the inside of the house become quite stuffy. Joseph Gellibrand said, "We are going on to Mr Swanson's first thing in the morning." He looked across at their hosts "is there a path we can follow to get there?"

"No need to look for a path Mr Gellibrand," Captain Pollock's exclaimed, "I'm sure John here won't mind taking you up the river on one of my stock horses," he said as he nodded and winked towards Aikers. Aikers looked up from his mug of rum, his mouth slightly agape, "Will you John?" Captain Pollock asked, his eyebrows raised. "It will take my men most of the morning to unload your Dray in any case," he went on.

"Ah, no, of course I won't mind Captain Pollock," Aikers stammered, as he glanced and nodded at Gellibrand and Hesse. The two lawyers nodded and smiled back through the thick drift of tobacco smoke.

"That would be very kind of you Mr Aikers," Gellibrand said with a friendly smile as more smoke drifted between them, "if we leave nice and early, we can have a good look around, as I understand it is not very far to Mr Swanston's station."

"No sir, an early start will be fine. It will give me time to get back here to my bullocks in the afternoon." Aikers agreed, and went back to studying the contents of his mug.

In the morning, the men toasted chunks of bread over the fire and drank sweet billy tea before they loaded their horses ready to continue the expedition. Captain Pollock walked to the edge of the river above the ford, before he wished the men well on their journey. Gellibrand and Hesse tipped their hats to Captain Pollock and thanked him enthusiastically for his hospitality at the station. Then, led by Aikers, they proceeded on horseback across the shallow ford and the horses climbed easily up the steep rocky bank on the other side.

From here the journey continued in a generally west to north-west direction, this time on the south-west side of the river with the steep hills to their left and the river on their right. From this side of the river they could see the expensive grassy plains that they had seen from the top of the hill and where they could now see the sheep of Captain Pollock grazing. They continued on, letting their horses set a fairly slow walking pace. Gellibrand continued to survey the land for productivity potential, occasionally stopping to dismount and dig slightly into the earth to check the soil quality and to study the grasses growing around there. Hesse continued to be awestruck and fascinated by the natural surroundings and excited at the prospect that he was one of the first men to ever explore this area.

By mid-morning the trio reached the point where the river wound tightly to the north and back again where a larger stand of river red gums appeared. The river was alive with wildlife here and the party regularly flushed kangaroos from the trees ahead as they approached. It appeared to the men that the animals here were not often disturbed by intruders. Hesse noticed that the large eagle was again circling way up high above them, riding effortlessly on the warm updraught of air, with a couple of crows following its' example. Going around and around right above their position on the ground. Gellibrand suggested that this was a good place to stop for a rest and a cup of tea.

They stopped and again Hesse went about collecting wood and making a fire for tea. However, as the grass here was thick and very dry, he was careful to clear an area before lighting the fire. And again, Gellibrand laid down for a rest and took more of his little white pills. Aikers sat on a log trying not to let his look of impatience be too apparent to these two gentlemen. The place where they rested, was very peaceful and shaded from the hot sun. The only sounds now were of the many species of birds that bounded in the trees and along the river, interspersed by the occasional croak of an unseen frog. However the men started to get a slight feeling of unease given that they were now getting well beyond the reach of what they thought as civilisation, although none of them spoke of this feeling.

When the men continued their journey on horseback following the meandering river they did not go far before they came to a junction. It appeared that a river went off to the south-west and another branch to the north. The men stopped and Gellibrand urged his horse forward to look across the river at the plains to the south-west. Aikers frowned and looked at Gellibrand's back and said "we need to go to the north-west sir, to get to Mr Swanson's run. It's this way," he went on gesturing ahead of his horse. Aikers sat on his horse looking across from Gellibrand to Hesse waiting for a response.

Gellibrand continued to sit on his horse looking the other way for a few minutes, before he finally turned back to the other men and said, "we are going to have a look on the other side of this river first." And he looked each man in the eye waiting to see if he would be challenged. He then went on "we have all day to get to Mr Swanson's, it won't hurt to have a look."

Aikers looked at Gellibrand, then he looked down at the ground for a minute while he scratched his head, and he said "Once we cross that river, we are in completely uncharted lands. Never explored by any white men before. And I also happen to know from the blacks around Geelong, and Captain Pollock's, that this is the boundary." He looked very seriously at Gellibrand and went on "This is the river even they will not cross, lest it be an act of war!"

"An act of war!" Gellibrand exclaimed in an almost mocking tone. "Surely you are being a bit dramatic Mr Aikers! It is obvious that there is no one around, who is going to know if we are to look around? Who is going to stop us if we have a look at those plains beyond the river? In any case if we see the blacks coming, we will simply return to this place. We can easily outrun men on foot, when we are on our horses"

Gellibrand sat forward on his horse looking directly at Aikers, his horse swaying slightly with its head down, as if it too were wondering which way they were going to go. Aikers responded "It is not that simple sir, you might only see one or two black fellows in the distance if you see someone coming, but they have eyes everywhere." He sat still looking Gellibrand straight in the eye. "And they can communicate across great distances, you might find yourself well outnumbered before you even know it."

"Don't be daft! How on earth can these primitive savages communicate? Do you think these people practice the voodoo magic of the islanders Mr Aikers?" Gellibrand said as he laughed at Aikers' comments. Hesse looked on, not saying anything, not sure what to think.

"Oh, they can communicate alright! I've heard all about it. When these black fellas see someone on their land, and they are only a small group they take the coals from their fire and throw them on their own huts. You see, they generally only have small fires for cooking, and their huts, or mia-mias as they call them, are just made up of sticks and bark. So when they set their huts on fire it sends up big plumes of white smoke and they can even throw a bit of green foliage on there to increase the smoke. This can be seen from many miles and other clans camped in the district will see the smoke and know that it is a sign of danger and for help." He looked from Gellibrand to Hesse for a response, but they both looked back at him with a puzzled expression. It appeared they had not thought of such a system.

Gellibrand as an experienced lawyer was not perturbed by having to influence someone to come around to his point of view. He persisted "We can just go a couple of miles beyond the river, if we see anyone or if we see any of these signal fires about which you speak, then we will instantly retreat to this junction in the river. We have come a very long way to see this land Mr Aikers. And I would greatly appreciate if you would continue to act as our guide." He continued to hold the gaze of Aikers, "and when we too are landholders in this area, I'm sure we can again avail ourselves of your services." He paused, and then he stated firmly, "Do you understand me, Mr Aikers?"

"So, just a couple of miles then?" Aikers responded, as he scratched his beard and again looked down at the ground. "I guess that will be all right, Mr Gellibrand, but we will have to take our time and keep our eyes wide open." He looked at the two gentlemen and saw the hint of a smile come across the face of young Hesse. "Come along the river a bit, until we find a place to cross." He kicked his horse up without looking back and turned left along the river that runs to the south-west. George Hesse again notice the little white coloured kestrel that hovered just overhead. They seemed very numerous in this area, and not afraid to come near the men. He puzzled a bit over this, and then followed the other men.

****

Here the landscape changed slightly, they had gone beyond the western end of the range of steep hills, and now what they saw appeared to be an ancient and very wide riverbed. With the hills on their left, and an escarpment a mile or so wide to their right, or the north, once forming the banks of that ancient river. And so before them to the west and south-west was again a massive open plain, only speckled with the odd eucalyptus tree. Gellibrand's mouth was almost watering at the site of this prime grazing country, and he had a feeling like butterflies in his stomach. He could see this as the ideal place to set up his own run for himself and his son.

John Aikers continued to lead them along the river to the south-west, looking for a suitable place to ford, but the river banks, while not particularly high, were very steep down to the water. So they continued for a while in that general south-westerly direction. They found however that after a while the river turned west away from the hills and the land opened up into vast flat land. Gellibrand told Aikers not to worry about crossing the river yet and instructed that they would just follow the river course and see where it led. They saw no people but continued at a slow pace and without saying anything it was clear, that each man was at least slightly on edge.

They stopped proceeding once again for Gellibrand to have a rest in the afternoon and this time Hesse also laid on the ground, resting and looking up at the sky. Again one of the little kestrels hovered only about 10 feet above, and Hesse watched it. He seemed to be looking into its eyes to see if he could see what the kestrel was hunting.

Aikers asked, without looking at anyone in particular, how far they were planning to go? Hesse looked to Gellibrand to respond and of course he did. "We will press on for maybe just another hour, there will still be plenty of time to get back to the river junction, and on to Mr Swanston's. The days are very long at this time of year." Aikers looked down at the ground kicking at a clod of dirt with his foot, and while he looked particularly uneasy, he did not object. In fact, he began to pack his things back in the saddlebags indicating he was ready to press on. He also was quite obvious when pulling his gun from its holster and checking that it was charged and ready to fire.

They continued on at a walking pace on their horses which were content to file along, Aikers in the lead, Gellibrand next and young Hesse taking up the rear. They saw nothing new as they headed further west, the long dry grass, the occasional kangaroo and lots of bird life. Across the river to the west the plane seemed endless. To the north they could now barely see the escarpment that was several miles away and to the south they could make out another range of hills many, many miles away. So far away in fact it was difficult to tell if it was in fact a range of hills, or dark grey clouds on the horizon.

As they came over a rise at a bend in the river a flat area of land below them formed a horse-shoe shape where the river swept around it, and before the adventurers realised it, they stumbled right into a camp-site. Aikers pulled his horse up so sharply that he surprised it, after many hours plodding, and it reared up slightly and almost threw him on the ground. "Fuck! Fuck... Fucking hell!" Aikers said as he pulled his gun from its holster, whirled his horse around and scanned the surroundings for any danger. Gellibrand also looked around but remained quite calm. His hand more discreetly went to the handle of a pistol in his belt. Hesse looked very startled and spun around swivelling in his saddle trying to look in every direction at once.

What they saw before them was a cleared area of land, at the centre of which was a well-used camp fire. There were black coals in the fireplace indicating a recent fire and the sandy ground right around it was bare of grass where many feet had tread. Not far from the fire was an unnatural hump that appeared to be formed by a combination of earth, ash and bones. Several large river stones and sheets of bark were also scattered around the cooking fire. Closer to the river, there were some very large stones in a pile that appeared to be a man-made arrangement.

"Don't panic gentlemen." Gellibrand said calmly but firmly, "There is no one around now." But having said that, the men, Gellibrand included, continued to sit silently for what seemed like a long time continually scanning the tree line and the river for any signs of the movement of men.

Below their position, was a flat area of clear land, and along this stretch the river formed a long wide pool with bright green reeds clustered on the near bank. There were a few large old gum trees and the far bank, which was much steeper than the near side, had a rocky outcrop at the top of the bank.

Eventually John Aikers turned his horse around and started to canter back past the other two men without speaking. "Where do you think you're going?" Gellibrand called loudly in what sounded like an exasperated tone. Aikers pulled his horse up and turned sideways to look back at the two lawyers, still both sitting still on their horses near the camp fire.

"We have to get the hell out of here Mr Gellibrand," he called back still looking around uneasily as though he may be attacked at any moment. "You would have to be mad to stay here another minute when it is plainly clear that there are black fellas about, and we don't know where the fuck they are."

Gellibrand sat still calmly on his horse, while George Hesse's horse shifted its weight uneasily as it could feel the tension in the skittery rider on its back. He said again, but more firmly, "There is no one around, and in any case, this gives us an advantage." Aikers looked at him in amazement, and Hesse too looked at him sideways with a furrowed brow but said nothing. "We know the local blacks have been here and gone. This fire is at least a few days old and we can clearly see that there is no one around now." He said with particular emphasis on the word "now". "If we scout around this area a bit, we can make absolutely sure that the blacks have moved on and it will be safe to carry on." He looked from Hesse to Aikers and back again. "We have guns, horses

123

and an intellect that far exceeds the capacity of a handful of savages to pose any great danger to us." And without looking at Aikers again, he instructed Hesse to scout along the river bank, and indicated that he would do a quick sweep of the grassy plane.

In fact, from this position, the men could see for a very long way in every direction. Across the river to the west, vast plains stretched out for miles, to the south-west the river valley only contained a few trees and clumps of native grass. To the east was also a grassy plane for a few miles until the large hills that formed the range back to Geelong, and back to the north-east the horizon was marked with a single large flat-topped mountain. The only movement the men could see in any direction, was the heat-haze rising steadily from the sun-baked earth.

The three riders came back together at the top of the rise after 10 or 15 minutes scouting around. "This rise over here" Gellibrand said as he pointed back to the south-east "would be a fine site for a homestead. This river is running high now, and it is the height of summer." He gazed down at the river deep in his own thoughts and did not appear to be waiting for a response from the other two men. "It would water stock right along this grassy plane, no problem at all."

Gellibrand pulled a journal from the pocket of his saddlebags and began to scratch notes with a pencil as he often did. "We really need to be getting back now Mr Gellibrand?" Aikers said with a tinge of annoyance in his voice. He looked to Hesse when Gellibrand ignored him and kept scribbling in his journal, but Hesse just raised his eyebrows and shrugged.

"I am far too tired to ride back to Swanston's station at this time of day." Gellibrand said in an even tone, not looking up from his journal "we can stay here the night, and map out 15 or 20 thousand acres around this site in the morning, and then head on to Swanston's." This was clearly meant as an order from Gellibrand and was not a question. Aikers was looking to Hesse again and shaking his head in exasperation.

"I agreed to take you to Swanston's station" Aikers said looking directly at Gellibrand who continued to write in his journal, "now we have ridden completely in the wrong direction and walked right into the hostile savages home camp. Even the savages back around Geelong tell us that there is a river to the west that even they will never cross for fear of the murderous bastards who live in the area beyond. I think this is that river and I don't plan to stay here another minute.

You gentlemen can keep going the wrong way, that is up to you." And even though Gellibrand ignored him Aikers pointed at the flat-topped mountain back in the direction from where they had ridden earlier. "That mountain with the flat top that you can see on the horizon." He glanced at Hesse and saw that he at least was paying attention, "that marks the direction you need to go to get back to the junction in the rivers, from there you just follow the river to the north-west. There is a stock track along that far bank that will take you straight to Swanston's station."

Both Aikers and Hesse sat silently staring at Gellibrand waiting for him to acknowledge what Aikers had just said. Gellibrand said nothing, but continued writing and sketching in his journal. After what seemed like minutes, George Hesse cleared his throat and timidly asked "Mr Gellibrand?"

"Yes, yes! The river to the north-east leads to Swanston's, the river we are on now, that leads straight back to Captain Pollock's." Gellibrand grumbled and looked up from his papers, "thank you for your assistance Mr Aikers, I am sure we can find our own way from here."

"Suit yourself sir." Aikers said as he wheeled his horse around to face back up the river, "it has been a pleasure to meet you gentlemen." He said to them both, but he nodded his head and touched the brim of his hat to young Hesse as he rode past, and he did not look back as he cantered his horse back over the rise and quickly he disappeared from sight.

As had become the unspoken practice, Hesse tethered the horses, gathered firewood and water, and prepared the camp site. While Gellibrand was a very intelligent man and respected lawyer, it was becoming apparent to George Hesse that he was no bushman, and probably not accustomed to having to take care of himself. Hesse soon had a fire made from the abundant dry twigs he had gathered and sat the billy of water at the edge of the fire to heat up. It felt a bit uneasy to George Hesse setting up camp right in the home of the Indigenous peoples, but it certainly was a beautiful place for a camp site.

Chapter nine

In the morning, George Hesse awoke with a terrible start, as a shadow passed across his eyes in the morning sunshine. He sat up with a gasp, but saw that it was just one of the little grey kestrels hovering about. He relaxed back into his rolled-up waistcoat and closed his eyes to the bright summer sun. Clearly sleeping near the camp of the natives had made him much more tense that he had previously been aware.

After the two men had eaten breakfast of salted pork, they prepared the horses for another full day of riding. Gellibrand called Hesse over to the clear area of dirt around the natives' camp fire where he brushed smooth an area with the flat edge of a long thin stick. "Look here young Hesse" he indicated in a friendly tone, as he scratched a winding line in the earth with the stick. "This is the river, where we have come thus far, from the junction," he continued to draw his dirt-map, "and here is the hill just behind us here. And this is where the river continues, through what I expect is more of the grassy plains like we can see across the river. So," he looked up at Hesse, to see if he was following, "assuming there is grazing land for at least two miles in each direction from the river, all we need to do is map the land for about five miles of river frontage, and we will have our fifteen to twenty thousand acres."

"That makes sense... I guess," George Hesse replied, scratching his head and tilting his hat back, as he examined the simple map.

"You know, you will profit greatly if you follow my example Mr Hesse," Gellibrand said, in his best fatherly voice. He looked George straight in the eye, "Always get in early, and take up all that you can. That is the value in these new frontiers. Don't wait until it is too late. You can just sell out later on if you find managing a sheep run is not for you."

The two men mounted up and rode at a walking pace along the contour of the hill from where they had an uninterrupted view over the river and the planes beyond. Although they did not speak of it, the men continually scanned the area for any signs of man. They saw nothing but the movement of kangaroos moving from the grassy areas where they had been grazing to the shade of the tress where they would rest for the hotter part of the day.

And it appeared to be shaping up to be an unusually hot day. Not only was the bright sun making them hot as it got higher into the morning sky, but the air was very humid as well. The men sweated heavily beneath their wide brimmed hats and their heavy English coats and the persistently annoying flies seemed to revel in the conditions. It was not long before George Hesse had stripped down to his light cotton shirt and he drank deeply from his canteen. Every half hour or less, Gellibrand would bring them to a halt, while he took out his journal to make a sketch-map of the area and to take notes.

Gellibrand and Hesse

By the time Gellibrand estimated that they had gone about five miles, as the crow flies, the river was significantly lower, and narrower then where they began. As usual, Gellibrand wanted to stop for a rest and tea. The humidity was clearly making him even more lethargic than usual.

From here they could see the ranges to the south more clearly than before. A long row of hills that stretched right along the horizon, maybe forty or fifty miles away they guessed. Out to the west the grassy plains continued, it seemed, forever. Only now the plains were marked by two small, but abrupt, hills that rose just few miles from where they had stopped. And further west, on the horizon, one or two more hills arose, unexpectedly from the surrounding flat land. Like rounded blemishes that had been plonked on what was otherwise an entirely unremarkable landscape. Also, to the west and to the north-west, dark storm clouds were quickly building, as the day got hotter and hotter, and the men grew more sweaty and uncomfortable.

"We can easily cross the river now Mr Hesse, between the pools here the river is barely flowing. And it has turned almost due south, and we still need to assess the land over the west bank." Gellibrand said, as he gestured with his chin, while looking at George Hesse. The two men were reclined under a shady gum tree on the hill on the east bank, looking across the river. Hesse looked away from his older companion at the gathering storm clouds that were moving now from the west along the northern horizon. As if to underline what Hesse was thinking, several pairs of large black cockatoos flew over their heads going south, screeching as they went, as though they were retreating to safety from the impending

129

storm.

Hesse had grown up in the country, and he had learnt from his father how to read the weather, and the terrain. Gellibrand noticed the young man's concern at the darkening sky, and he stated, "Don't worry about the clouds, a bit of rain might cool this intolerable heat!"

"No sir, I think this storm is going to go around us." He looked across at Gellibrand, who was a bit surprised to hear young George finally express his own view. "The clouds built up in the west, but it is going away to the north. And earlier there was no wind at all, and now there is a slight breeze coming up from the south east, but it is swirling around. Very unsettled." He concluded, shaking his head in a puzzled expression as he continued to look at the black clouds in the northern sky.

The men easily picked their way across the shallow river on the horses, although they paused for quite a while for the horses to drink as they too were suffering from the heat and humidity under the weight of riders and their kits. They headed west across the grassy plain which here had more frequently scattered rocks and large exposed rocky outcrops. There remained no obvious sign of any human presence on this side of the river, and in the blaring heat, very little in the way of animal or bird life either. It was hard for young George Hesse to imagine why any living soul would be out in this totally exposed landscape in such oppressive conditions.

As he thought this the first flash of lightning caught the attention of the men, away over their right shoulders. The sky was now almost equally divided in a line running east to west. Dark angry storm clouds in the north, and a clear blue sky above the men in the south. It looked as though the band of storm clouds was following the escarpment that formed the northern bank of the main river valley that they had followed until they deviated at the river junction. The horizon now indistinguishable between the blue hills of the river bank and the blue-black clouds that swirled and built up above. A large V-shape of grey from the clouds to the ground indicated to Hesse that rain was falling at that place far to the north.

The men ploughed on. Gellibrand continued to sketch and take notes. He stopped periodically to turn over a clod of earth and examine the soil. The two men both continually turned their faces to the right to watch the impressive storm move across the northern sky. Now large and frequent bolts of lightning flashed from the clouds-to-clouds and at times clouds-to-ground. But it was so far away that the low rumble of thunder followed some seconds in delay. It was making the horses spook and they whinnied and snorted in apparent dissatisfaction at the storm.

When the men stopped for lunch that day, under a lone gum tree on the plain, they could no longer see the landmarks that made out the river course. The air had become hazy and the sun obscured by the thick clouds made the horizons dark in all directions. The continually shifting wind made the men and horses even more uneasy as they day went on. After they ate, the two explorers lay down and slept in the shade of the tree to recover their strength.

****

Hesse again woke from a deep slumber with a start, but this time for good reason. Plumes of grey smoke wafted all around and the horses whinnied and stomped at the ground with their hooves. Hesse jumped to his feet and looked about. Not only was smoke wafting about, but black ash of burnt leaves and grass was floating down from the sky as well.

Without thinking, young Hesse kicked Gellibrand in the leg to wake him up. Gellibrand woke up grumbling but quickly became silent and his mouth hung open and he too gazed about at the scene of smoke and ash raining down. "Quick, get on your horse," Gellibrand commanded as he threw the saddle over his own steed and pulled up the girth straps. His horse shifted uneasily and blew air from its nostrils with impatience. Hesse had quickly prepared his own mount and as he put his left foot in the stirrup and lifted himself over the saddle his horse was already moving off instinctively away from the smoke.

The men let the horses canter to the west as this was slightly uphill and it appeared that the smoke was less thick than downhill to the east. The wind had swung to the north-west while they slept and now the stiff hot wind pushed the smoke towards the south-east. They soon got up out of the thick smoke and Gellibrand pulled them to a halt and they both turned the horses to the north to survey the situation. About a mile away they could see the glow of the flames through the white-grey smoke that was being pushed along to their right by the wind. The grass-fire made a long arc over many miles from the north right around to the east from where they now watched. In the north there were larger bursts of flames where gum trees ignited into fire balls, and to the far east new flames burst forth in the grass where hot embers floated down ahead of the main fire front.

Hesse looked across at the older man. Gellibrand sat with his mouth hanging open and his face as ashen and white as the smoke that now expanded into a massive plume that reached to the sky where it began to form a cloud. "We have to keep moving this way Mr Gellibrand!" He exclaimed in a loud voice, "to get out of the path of the fire. The wind is blowing it from the north-west, we have to go to the south-west and hope to God it passes by, then we can go back to the river after the fire-front has passed by." He paused but Gellibrand kept staring into the fire, "Come on man!" he shouted this time, and finally the older lawyer looked and nodded, for Hesse to lead the way.

They cantered to the south-west for only about 20 minutes, but the shifting and gusting north wind was creating spot fires in all directions. Hesse pulled his horse up and Gellibrand's horse followed. Hesse sat still and studied the wind and the sky. "What is it Hesse, what are you doing?" Gellibrand asked in a frantic voice, but Hesse continued to gaze at a low hill to the west and again at the sky. Gellibrand followed Hesse's gaze, but could see nothing but smoke and ash.

"We have to go that way," Hesse said, pointing to the hill in the west.

"What? Why?" Gellibrand exclaimed, "The fire is about to sweep right through here, we have to go south, and outrun it."

"Don't you see?" young George Hesse asked the older man, "The ducks and the swans." He pointed again to the low hill before them, and this time Gellibrand saw what Hesse had been looking at. Flocks of water birds and several pairs of

133

swans flew around above that area, and then some took off towards the south. "There must be a large swamp or body of water just beyond that rise." And without waiting for Gellibrand to respond, he kicked up his horse and headed straight for the southern end of the low hill. Gellibrand followed close behind, keeping his head down low to avoid the smoke and ash in his eyes.

As they came over the rise the land dropped down and the ground was noticeably softer and the grass much greener. Overhead now large flocks and ducks, coots and other waterbirds were retreating south, following this depression in the earth, which appeared to be a wide swamp or watercourse that was now almost dry. Or it was just the edge of a much larger body of water that they could not see for all the smoke that had reduced visibility to not much more than a hundred yards or so. Hesse started to walk his horse up this wide depression to the north, to find the water, but just as they moved that way, a large stand of gum trees, maybe ten acres or more in area, burst into flames ahead of them.

It was an eerie sight, in the poor visibility of the now thick smoke, a wall of intense flames erupted that was a couple of hundred yards wide. But at the same time, the north wind all but disappeared. The smoke that was blowing in their faces started to rise up into the sky, and to clear from the ground level, providing some respite to the hot and exhausted men. They could go no further forward. And to either side was long dry grass. "I think we have found as safe a place as any," Hesse said calmly, as he dismounted from his horse, and stood watching the wall of fire a couple of hundred yards away from them.

Gellibrand dismounted as well, and leading his horse, walked up to stand beside Hesse. The fire no longer advanced but burned high and fierce in the small eucalypt forest. Hesse looked about, they stood in an area with tufts of long dry grass, but underneath the shorter grass was green, indicating that this was a swamp in winter, and must be still damp underneath. Hesse pointed to an area with the least amount of long grass, where water had pooled in the winter, "We should sit it out there, in that clearing." He said "The wind has died right off. Hopefully the fire will burn itself out in time." He led his horse the short distance to that area, and sat on a log, still holding the horse's reigns, "But we should keep the horses saddled and ready, in case we have to move fast." he said, determinedly.

As they watched the wall of fire over the next half hour, it slowly enveloped each tree in the small forest. Each time bursting into another inferno that leapt high into the air. It was an impressive and mighty sight, but the fire did not advance at all into the damp swamp area, and there was no wind. If anything, the men could now feel a very slight breeze of air going towards the fire, not towards them anymore, and they relaxed slightly, feeling that the main danger was now past.

As the men sat and watched the fire, they talked about what might be beyond these trees, from where all the water birds had come ahead of the fire. They determined that they would explore the body of water, once it was safe to move, before heading back to the main river, and then on the Swanston's Station. Then a strange thing happened.

Many dozens of crows had been disturbed by the fire and were flying all about the plains in an apparent chaotic and uncoordinated fashion. But now the crows all began to converge on the area between the men and the fire front. They swirled about and cawed loudly, still uncoordinated in flight, but forming one large mass, like a cloud of criss-crossing flapping black missiles. The crows, having formed this mass of hundreds of birds, then turned and all at once started swarming down the old watercourse towards, over and around the two men. Such was the startle and the sight to the two explorers, that they involuntarily ducked their heads and covered their faces with their arms, as the crows swooped and flapped co close as they passed by.

Within a minute or two, the crows had moved past the men and the oscillating black cloud moved away from them, to the south, on the same path the waterbirds and followed earlier in the day. As the men looked from the crows to each other, a roaring sound from the fire again caught their attention. They turned back to the fire and stood up, as the flames suddenly increased dramatically in size and intensity, again stretching way up into the sky with renewed but unexplained vigour. Then, so fast that the men could not even see what had happened, the fire was all around them.

Hesse instinctively threw his arm across his eyes as he felt the burn of the heat and smoke simultaneously on his face, in his nostrils, mouth and lungs. He could hear nothing but the roar of fire, feel nothing but burning, and could not open his eyes. His throat and lungs burnt but he could not hold his breath as he gasped for oxygen in what he thought may be his lasts seconds on earth.

Gellibrand and Hesse

All he could feel of his surroundings, was his horse pulling him along by the reigns, and it was only then that he became aware that he was running, but he did not know in what direction, and he felt pain and burning in is ankles as his socks melted into his skin. He had both hands trying to hold the reigns and his face buried down between his upper arms to guard from the intense burning all around him. He stumbled forward as the horse tried desperately to bolt from the flames, and Hesse tried desperately to stop it. He then became aware that his shirt was being pulled in the opposite direction. Gellibrand was clinging to his shirt tails.

All at once, Hesse crashed shins-first over a fallen log and Gellibrand crashed down on top of his back. He rolled face up and he felt then that the very strong gust of the north wind that had blown the fire onto them, had almost as quickly, moved the fire passed them. He sat up and looked around. Only the few scattered tufts of dry grass were burning quietly, and white smoke swirled all about, but the heat and intensity had already gone, and the smoke cleared quickly. He breathed in the clean air but felt the tightness in his throat from the burn it had just received. His eyes stung terribly from the assault of the hot air and smoke. Other than that, and some pain in his ankles and shins, Hesse appeared relatively unharmed, and relieved that he had survived being engulfed by fire.

Hesse helped to pull Gellibrand to his feet, the older man still looked frightened and confused. All about them burnt ground with tufts of smouldering grass dotted across miles of bare black ash. Hesse looked about in every direction, "The horses have bolted." He looked at the tracks on the ground, "they kept going that way" he said, pointing along the line of the tracks going due west. Gellibrand too looked around. Behind them, the dry grass was burning, to the north the gum tree forest still blazed, and to the west was open burnt ground where the fire had just gone through.

"Well, we may as well go and find them." He looked at George Hesse, "It is the only safe way to go anyway, where the fire has already burnt. And we have nothing without the saddlebags. No water, or food. No long-arms." And with that, Gellibrand set off across the freshly burnt earth. Hesse stood for a moment and blinked the soot out of his eyes. He was dismayed that the older man had said nothing of their miraculous survival, nor did he discuss what to do next. Then he obediently followed Gellibrand, off further into the unknown.

****

After walking for two hours, the men's' throats had become baked dry. They had initially followed the tracks of the horses across the fresh carpet of black ash, but they had lost the tracks once they had walked beyond the black corridor left by the wildfire. Following the thunderstorm that had started the fire, the wind had dropped and a brief heavy shower of rain had passed through. The rain was not enough to get a drink but was enough to wet their clothes and make them even more uncomfortable. The two men now staggered on aimlessly on the open plain of hard brown earth and dry brown grass. Trees were very few and far between and there was nothing much in the way of geography other than the odd hill that abruptly rose from the otherwise flat and barren landscape.

The men had not spoken for a long time, since they lost the tracks of the horses and left the danger of the fire behind them. They thought of nothing but water, as the sun burnt into their faces as it crept down toward the horizon ahead of them. They crossed a couple of minor creeks that ran north-south, but they were so shallow that they were bone dry at this time of year. Even though it seemed hopeless to walk on aimlessly, they had committed so much time to following the horses in this direction that they ploughed on slowly. It would take them a whole day or more to walk all the way back to the main river, and without having to say anything both men knew they could not make it without carrying water. The choice had been to walk on in a direction where they *might* find water, or turn back and walk over land where they already knew there was no water.

As the men pressed on the land became rockier, and there were low rises of rocky outcrops breaking the monotony of the open plains. As they slowly ambled up and over one of these rocky rises the sight beyond made them stop in their tracks and gape for a moment, before turning and breaking a slight smile to each other. What they saw was a round pool of water almost big enough to call a small lake, about two chain across. It was obviously larger and deeper in the winter as was evidenced by the chain or so of dry lake-bed that circled the whole body of water, with a crackled black crust. The water looked cool, blue and was only slightly rippled by the light breeze blowing into their faces.

Without speaking Gellibrand wrestled off his jacket, threw it to the ground and onto that tossed his hat. Hesse had already taken off, loping down across the dry lake-bed towards the inviting cool water, throwing his hat into the air with glee as he went. Young George Hesse had a smile from ear-to-ear as he approached the water with Gellibrand close on his heels.

Hesse stopped about a yard short of the water's edge and flopped down onto his knees, half laughing, and half sobbing with relief. Then two things happened simultaneously. Hesse recoiled backwards and met with the force of Gellibrand's knees as he was so close behind him as he eagerly approached the water also. And what had made Hesse recoil continued to fly straight at his face.

What Hesse saw as he dropped to his knees was a round white disc right in front of him. And that round white disc was the wide-open mouth of a snake about to strike. The next few milliseconds seemed to occur to Hesse in slow motion. He became aware that the thing coming forward at a speed he could not avoid was a snake with its mouth pulled so far open that the upper and lower jaw formed an almost straight vertical plane so that he could not see the head at all. The body was fat and about four-foot long coming out of the shallow water, with very prominent scales that made diamond patterns on its back. The body was a dark brown colour that was so similar to the colour of the lake-bed that Hesse had not seen the snake at all until it moved. The brown skin now glistened with copper tones in the sunlight as the contracted muscles released with all their power to propel the mouth and fangs of the venomous reptile right onto the left cheek of George Hesse.

Gellibrand danced backwards when Hesse pushed back from his knees against the older man flapping wildly at his face with both hands. Gellibrand did not know what on earth was wrong with Hesse for a moment until he too became startled by the large snake that, as soon as it dropped back to the ground, slithered very quickly across the bare lake-bed and retreated into the dry grass beyond. Where the snake probably would have been happy to go back to without incident, had Hesse seen it in time drinking at the water's edge, and allowed it to return to the safety of the grass unhindered.

Gellibrand stood dumbstruck by what had so suddenly occurred. He looked from the grass where the snake had disappeared, to young Hesse who writhed around on the ground clutching and scratching at his face like he was trying to physically pull something that was no longer there from his cheek.

"Stop it man!" Gellibrand croaked, through his throat so dry it was painful to speak, "let me have a look," he said as he knelt down and tenderly took hold of Hesse by each wrist. Gellibrand was afraid of what he might see, so he very slowly removed Hesse's trembling hands from his face and squinted his own eyes as though that might lessen the horror. What he saw was far less horrific in its appearance, but no less horrific in what it foretold.

Hesse had two puncture wounds, a bit less than an inch apart, just below the line if his cheekbone on the left side of his youthful face. The wounds were slightly torn and bleeding from where Hesse had ripped the snake from its purchase deep within his skin where it had pumped its full load of highly toxic venom. "Wash that off, son," Gellibrand croaked softly, and Hesse could see from the look on the man's face, and the soft tone of his usually gruff manner, that he thought the situation was very grim. "Have a drink and then I'll fix that up for you," he went on, as he pointed uncertainly at the wound on Hesse's cheek.

****

Hesse knelt at the edge of the small lake and spooned water over his face with both hands. He closed his eyes as he felt the now luxurious cool liquid wash over his face and down the front of his shirt. He drank very small amounts that he sucked from the palm of his hand as the cool shock to his stomach brought the pang of cramps. With his eyes shut, Hesse thought to himself, *this can't be happening, the snake can't have poisoned me, after all I've just been through to survive this far....* He knelt, beside the water, like he was praying or meditating for quite some time.

When Hesse finally opened his eyes and looked around, Gellibrand was sitting on the bank, very seriously scrutinising the blades on a small pocket-knife that he turned over in his hands. The knife was a typical pocket-knife of the time, with a bone handle and two folding blades, with one longer than the other. Gellibrand was feeling the keenness of one blade with his thumb, before folding that in, and trying the keenness of the other, and then opening both blades and repeating the process. He was procrastinating to avoid what he knew had to be done.

"Come and sit down here son," Gellibrand called softly to Hesse, and gestured with his hand. He tried a half-hearted smile to reassure young George that it was all okay. Hesse rose from his knees, walked over and sat cross-legged before Gellibrand and met his concerned eyes. Gellibrand held his hand open, with the pocket-knife laid open on his palm. He looked from the knife to Hesse hoping that it would be self-explanatory to the young man, what had to be done. The innocent and naive look on George Hesse's face stated it was not.

The two men sat for a moment, looking plainly into each other's eyes. "I have to open up the bite George," Gellibrand said, he looked down at the blade and avoided the reaction on the young man's face. "I have to cut it open, to bleed the poison out."

He looked up into the frightened wide eyes of Hesse, who looked from Gellibrand's face, down at the blade of the knife, and back again, his mouth open like he wanted to speak, but nothing came out. "It is the only way son," Gellibrand said "to stop the spread of the poison to your heart. I will be really quick, and you can wash it out straight away with water. Then hold this," he held out a relatively clean hand kerchief that he pulled from his pants pocket, "over the cut."

Hesse took in, held, then let out a very long quavering breath. He looked up into Gellibrand's now kind and sympathetic eyes, "Alright," he said firmly, "Just do it."

****

Gellibrand quickly drew the knife blade across the cheek of Hesse and split the skin across the 2 puncture marks. The cut was not very deep, but as with most head wounds, it began to bleed profusely. Hesse tried instinctively to put his hands over the wound, but Gellibrand swiftly took him by the wrists again, and lowered the young man's arms back down to his lap. Hesse began to sob quietly, with his head hung low, blood dripped down onto his ankle and boots and he looked like a sad child, sat cross legged and forlorn. He made little sound, but his shoulders bobbed and Gellibrand released Hesse's hands into his lap and patted him on the shoulder, and looked around to avoid the uncomfortable silence.

At the high water mark a bit further around the small lake, what had once been a large old tree was now just a tall white-grey trunk with a few large fallen limbs scattered about on the ground on the dry edge of lake bed. Further on again, from the dead tree, was something else laying on the ground, that to Gellibrand looked like it might be a dead kangaroo, but it didn't quite look right so he could not tell. This was about all Gellibrand could see, just the small lake and the grassy plane otherwise. Gellibrand strolled over to the dead tree, he kicked at the fallen sticks and branches and thought to himself, that at least there was plenty of dry fallen wood for a fire.

Then he wandered down toward what looked like the body of a kangaroo. He looked back and saw young Hesse still sitting on the ground with his head hung low. As he got closer to the kangaroo he realised why it looked odd. Both back legs had been neatly butchered from the body, and the tail had also been cut off. This just left the head and torso laying on the bare earth. Flies buzzed about the body, but it still looked fresh and had barely started to decompose. Gellibrand then noticed that there was a long straight stick on the ground, with a freshly snapped end. This must have been a spear used to kill the kangaroo, that had been discarded when the end broke off in the killing of the animal.

This all processed quickly in Gellibrand's mind. People, albeit savage blacks, had been here only one, or at the most, two days ago. There was a chance he could find these people and get a message out to rescue Hesse, and of course, himself. He walked to the edge of the grassy plain and there he saw in the crushed dry grass the footprints of two or three people, with bare feet, heading pretty much due south. So fresh were the tracks that even to the inexperienced tracking eye of this lawyer, he could plainly see the prints and the flattened dry grass in a straight path for some way into the distance.

Gellibrand simultaneously felt a flush of hope go through him, that he may find help for the otherwise doomed young man that he had brought into this wilderness, while at the same time a deep dread of having to willingly approach these barbaric blacks. He knew that he had no choice, so with renewed energy he strode back to where young Hesse was still sitting on the ground.

"Mr Hesse," Gellibrand said, and the young man looked up, a pitiful sight with tears in his eyes and the blood on his face already drying and no longer running from the superficial cut. "See that 'roo over there," and Hesse turned in the direction Gellibrand pointed, but said nothing, "It was speared by the blacks, only yesterday I would estimate, from the state of the carcass." George Hesse frowned and looked from the kangaroo carcass to the old lawyer and back, trying to understand what Gellibrand was getting at. Did he think they could eat the meat from the kangaroo?

He saw the puzzled look on the young man's face, and he stated plainly, "I'm going after them Hesse! I'm going to find the blacks." Hesse's eyes opened wide with realisation, with the hope that Gellibrand shared for finding help for them both. "They might have a camp not far from here." He paused as he gazed off to the south, "And I can pay one or two of the black boys to go and get help." He looked back down at Hesse's now hopeful eyes, "You know those little buggers travel many miles over-land in one day. Why I bet they could get back to the nearest station by tomorrow to bring help."

Gellibrand spent 15 minutes making Hesse as comfortable as he could before heading off. He sat Hesse at the base of the dead tree where he had a bit of shade and could rest back against a log formed by one of the fallen limbs. He rolled up Hesse's jacket for padding against the hard wood. Hesse still looked fine, apart from the messy wound on his face, but Gellibrand knew that time was against them as he had heard plenty of stories about the lethality of the snakes both here and in Van Diemen's Land.

Gellibrand had no way of carrying water, so he knelt by the water and took many small sips before he stood up and brushed himself off. "I'll be back soon," he said to George Hesse, who forced a small but unconvincing smile. "Keep drinking water and washing that cut to keep it open and clean." he advised Hesse, although many little black flies were already crawling on his face and buzzing about annoying the young man.

"I'll be fine sir," Hesse said stoically, nodding to the older man, who looked down doubtfully.

The shadows had grown very long by the time Gellibrand strode out onto the plane, but the angle of the sun at least made the tracks that he followed through the grass easy to make out. As Gellibrand walked along, now clear of the intense situation with Hesse, he became aware of how exhausted he was, and how much he wished to lay back against a log and rest himself. He knew he had to put his exhaustion out of his mind, and just hope that the camp of the blacks would not be too far away, and he could at least reach them before dark.

After following the tracks through the dry grass for about 20 minutes or so they led to one of the minor dry creek beds and then disappeared. The surface of the dry creek bed was too hard to reveal footprints and was devoid of grass, but as the creek ran roughly north-south he thought it safe to assume that the people whose tracks he followed had continued south, following the dry creek. As Gellibrand walked the dry creek bed the light was beginning to fade, but it was still hot as only a soft northerly breeze was blowing on his back. He wondered what he could say, or how he could approach the blacks, so as to avoid them attacking him. They might never have seen an Englishman before, he thought to himself.

The landscape changed slightly as he walked south between two of the short sharp hills he had seen in the distance earlier in the day. There were more of the scattered gum trees and the banks of the dry creek rose a bit higher than before, giving the impression that he was heading downstream, and hopefully he thought, towards where there might be water. As he was thinking about this his heart suddenly jumped as he saw ahead, just over the right bank of the creek, the small glow of a camp fire. He immediately felt the contradiction of excitement and apprehension at having located the blacks.

****

Gellibrand followed the small glow of the camp fire as he walked along the bank of the dry creek. The orange glow was in clear contrast to the land in the fading sunlight. It was very hard for him to tell how far away the fire was, as it was just a single bright dot in the distance across the flat land. Was it the glow of a small fire not far away, he thought? Or the glow of a large fire a long way off? And the fire sometimes disappeared completely from view as he walked, which he assumed meant that there were trees or something else between him and the fire that at times obscured his view as he moved along the wide flat creek bed.

When Gellibrand came to a high point on the creek bank where he thought he would finally be able to see the camp, to which the fire light had led him, he could not see anything of the glow at all. Gellibrand plonked himself down on a large rock perplexed at how he had lost sight of the light that logically could only have been from a man-made camp fire. He sat, with his head bowed and looked at the sandy ground between his feet and wondered what to do next, but when he looked up, he saw the glow of the fire-light again, but straight ahead down the creek-bed this time. The light was as bright and as obvious as before, and Gellibrand was unable to understand how he had thought he had come to the source on this bank, when it was so clearly visible another 30 degrees east of where he had been heading before and probably still half a mile further.

Gellibrand again ambled along the creek bed with renewed vigour. It was getting quite dark by this time and he wanted badly to reach the camp of the blacks before it was too late to send help back for Hesse. Again, the firelight was a single amber glow in the distance that appeared, disappeared and flickered. Although Gellibrand was completely exhausted, he just kept his focus on the point of the glowing light so that this time he would not lose his course. As he walked, he imagined that the light flickered as men danced around the fire obscuring the view as they moved in front of the flames. Gellibrand's mind conjured a scene where savages performed a ritual killing, where he was the sacrificial lamb around whom the savages danced in the flickering light of the camp fire. Rather than being fearful now, Gellibrand smiled and chuckled out loud to himself. Instead of hiding from danger, he was now determined to walk right into the lair of the heathen cannibals.

****

George Hesse sat up with his back against a large log that was light grey from years of sun and water. His legs stretched out before him pointed to the water only a few yards away. A light north wind blew gently through his sandy blonde hair and the warmth of the low sun on his face confirmed his decision that he did not need to light a fire. Anyway, he did not want to move or do anything that might speed the poison through his veins any faster than it already would have been spreading.

Hesse barely moved a muscle, just his eyes slowly flickered as he looked about. Where he had previously felt pain in his face, in his aching legs, in his hungry stomach, now had all become just numb. It was his mind that had become the focus of all attention. His mind raced around the various scenarios that might be the final fate of this young adventurer. Hesse just let his mind wander without any great fear or trepidation, as his eyes watched the reflections on the lightly ruffled water. His head hung slightly sideways rested back against the large fallen tree, his whole body limp with total exhaustion.

Time slipped by, and Hesse had barely been aware of his surroundings, contemplating instead his own fate. He lifted his head to look around, realising that it had started to get dark and that perhaps he would survive into this dark night. Alone but still alive. He could not imagine that Gellibrand would have been able to find help and return before nightfall now. The shadows from tufts of grass that were speckled on the west bank of the waterhole now cast long shadows across the bare earth to the water.

Over both his left and right shoulders, the closest not more than a chain away and staring straight at him, were quite a few kangaroos. Large grey beasts mostly with a few young ones and a couple of reddish-brown specimens too. Hesse was surprised that in his deep meditations he had not even heard all these kangaroos' approach and from where they had come he had no idea. A couple of the kangaroos grazed, bent over and resting on front paws while they chewed at dry grass. But as he looked at each of the other large animals, they stared straight back at him, they barely moved other than to flick an ear, to remove an annoying fly.

All of a sudden, the scene of the waterhole became a mass of colour and noise, lit bright with green and yellow hues. A large flock of brilliant green budgerigars had landed at the water's edge, and some perched along another fallen tree limb in a long line of identically marked birds. The low sun and otherwise colourless landscape made the bright colours of the small birds an extreme and impressive contrast. The dull colour of the fallen limb and the brown earth had become almost invisible in the failing light and the long line of brightly coloured birds seemed almost to float in the dusty air. Despite his dire circumstances, young Hesse could not help but be awestruck by this natural wonder and to feel his spirits lift at the sight before him. His mouth twitched into the slightest smile as he gazed at the natural beauty that had appeared out of nowhere.

The appearance of the birds had made Hesse contemplate that this spot was probably a reliable water source in this otherwise large and dusty barren area where birds and animals would be able to come each evening to drink. That was why the kangaroos had stood away in the grass staring at him. Hesse had stopped the kangaroos from coming to their usual drinking spot and they stared waiting for him to move away. In fact, when he looked back over at the kangaroos to his right, one of the larger animals, a female with a bulging pouch hanging in front, had crept a few yards closer, and appeared to be sniffing at the air to work out if Hesse was a danger or not.

The sun slowly disappeared below the horizon and Hesse gazed at the changing colours of the sky, from the orange glow of the sunset, to the purple and then deep, dark blue of the opposite end of the sky. Hesse laid his head back and gazed into the deep darkening sky waiting for sleep and the night to pass. Holding on dearly to hope that he would survive until Gellibrand returned with help.

Hesse was woken suddenly when he was startled by sensing a presence close up to his face. The sky was a very deep black by that time but speckled with thousands of stars. He looked around, but all about was very dark then. All he could see, other than the stars in the night sky, was the reflection of the glittering stars on the water. Against that reflection, when his eyes had adjusted to the light, Hesse could make out a silhouette. There was a kangaroo very close to him, so close he could feel its breath and hear the snuffling of its nose as it was sniffing him. Then there was a sudden "thump" very close and the kangaroo itself jumped back a pace and Hesse became aware of other animals nearby that startled and moved at the sound also. Like a rabbit, the kangaroo had thumped its foot close to Hesse in an apparent effort to make him move, or reveal himself, as the curious animals still tried to work out what this intruder was that had failed to move away and clear the waterhole for other thirsty animals to drink.

Hesse was by then too tired to react but was bemused by the antics of the kangaroo, that he pictured in his mind as likely being the same female that was approaching closer in the daylight hours. Her warning shot had startled other animals and made Hesse aware that the setting sun had not been the end of the activity, but just another beginning. He could see other animals, probably more kangaroos, passing between him and the water, just within a couple of yards, against the reflection of the stars on the water. The fear the animals held about the unidentified intruder had eventually been overcome by extreme thirst from the hot dusty weather.

After a while there was another change in the immediate environment of the waterhole where Hesse lay wide awake. Some clouds had come across the sky and it had become even darker than before. The warm breeze had swung to the southwest and lowered the temperature just slightly. Just cool enough to send a little shiver through Hesse's body after the great heat of the day. The kangaroos that had quietly milled about the waterhole, for what seemed to Hesse like hours, all thumped noisily away to his right across the open plains until out of earshot and Hesse felt alone again.

As Hesse lay staring into the starry night, he picked up for the first time a new sound that he had not heard among the mob of kangaroos, if it had been present at all before now. He could hear a distinct gnawing sound and muffled breathing. Looking toward the sound revealed nothing in the dark but as he focussed he could picture in is mind what it was. While he concentrated on the sound and listened, he realised that something was eating the remains of the kangaroo carcass that Gellibrand had earlier pointed out further around the edge of the waterhole.

Dingoes did not exist in Van Diemens Land and so Hesse had never seen them himself. He could then only imagine what was going on as the wild dogs became more ravenous in their eating. The dingoes noisily tore at the flesh of the kangaroo and he felt knots in his own stomach when he heard the dogs crunching up the bones of the dead animal with powerful jaws and the occasional yelp as the dogs fought over the best position from which to feast. Hesse could not help but wonder, if he lay here long enough, or became sick and helpless, would these gregarious carnivores turn on him next?

Chapter ten

Sunlight had already hit the tops of the tall eucalyptus trees when Gellibrand opened his right eye. His left eye was pressed against the sand as he lay face down on the bank of the creek among soft tufts of grass. His throat was so dry it was hard to swallow and as he sat up his stomach growled with hunger. It was a moment before the anxiety gripped him again as he remembered that young Hesse was still alone and out there waiting for rescue. Gellibrand got to his feet and walked to a lone tree a few yards away to urinate. It was then that he looked about and saw that on a rise just a couple of hundred yards away a thick column of smoke from a freshly stoked fire rose straight up into the clear morning air.

There was no mistaking it this time, there was human habitation just minutes away from where he had finally collapsed chasing the illusive firelight the night before. He still could not comprehend how a distinct light had appeared, moved, disappeared, reappeared and led him to this place without ever catching up to find what was the source of the light. In any case, he had found a camp now and he would have to face whatever fate would bring when he presented to the local inhabitants.

As he emerged from the trees along the creek bed Gellibrand found that there was a small lake of maybe five acres in area and almost perfectly round between him and a small hill. The lake was surrounded by low vegetation and reeds, and throughout the entire lake were large nests of dry reeds and twigs built by the many dozens of black swans that drifted about on the water. There were also numerous varieties of ducks, coots and other waterfowl that made the small lake look like a picture of a perfect environment to produce food for the local people. No doubt this had also been the refuge for at least some of the waterbirds that Gellibrand had previously seen fleeing south ahead of the wildfire.

As Gellibrand skirted around the edge of the small lake he headed towards the hill from where the smoke he had observed appeared to be rising. The hill was almost bare of trees but had a large rocky outcrop around the top that created a natural shelter from the prevailing winds of the south-west. Soon Gellibrand saw that there were several people walking about the camp fire, busily collecting some things from about the camp area. There were maybe only half a dozen men and a couple of women from what Gellibrand could make out. They appeared to be gathering and packing up their possessions as if ready to move camp. One young man, almost naked in the warm morning sun, but with a skin rug slung over one shoulder, spotted Gellibrand approaching and pointed as he called out to his companions, who all stopped what they were doing at once and stared at the strange man approaching the camp.

Gellibrand and Hesse

Gellibrand continued to steadily walk up the hill into the camp area, with his hands spread wide, palms up, in a sign of his peaceful intentions. He still had a pistol tucked into his belt, but he saw no need to remove that as he thought that the savages would have no idea that it was a weapon anyway. The men all stood their ground, some with spears in their hands, but none pointed the spears or otherwise threatened to stop the approaching foreigner. The men and women all stared at him in silence, just exchanging quick glances between themselves with curious expressions on their faces.

The young man who was closest to his approach, the same young man who had first seen Gellibrand, eventually called out something that he could not understand, so the white man stopped where he was, just a few yards away. "My name is Joseph Gellibrand" he announced, in his formal barrister's tone, as he looked about the faces of the men nearest to him, but he was given no reaction. He thought he should take a more simple approach "Me" he said and pointed to his own chest "Me Jo" again pointing at himself. The men looked sideways at each other, slightly amused. "I…. That is we… need your help" he continued, then pointing more vigorously at himself and away in the direction whence he came.

The men continued to stand still, and just gazed at this strange fellow, who persisted again, "Me Jo", he said, with an imploring look to the man closest, then Gellibrand was started to bang his chest in frustration.

"I know!" Came the response that almost knocked Gellibrand off his feet with surprise. The voice that had answered him in English came not from the young man, but from a woman sitting down by the fire. She had been quietly placing things in a string bag as he approached and only now did he look properly at her face, and into the eyes that directly met his gaze. The eyes of Murnin, Jacky's wife from the Exe River run.

Gellibrand walked past the young man, who did not challenge him, and he squatted down near Murnin. "Hello Murnin", he said "what are you doing way out here?" He asked, in a croaky voice. Murnin said something to one of the young men, and he then brought Gellibrand a wooden bowl of water. Then she looked Gellibrand in the eyes, with a rather blank expression.

"Because of you, our family was all killed. Because of you, I was taken away to be the wife of another man," Murnin said in a cold voice, no emotion on her face. She went back to packing up and tying up the string bag of utensils.

"I heard about the trouble Murnin, and I am sorry, but it was not my fault." Gellibrand said, between sips of the cool fresh water from the bowl. Murnin did not look up, she just shrugged slightly, and went about what she was doing. "I will do what I can to restore you to your previous position Murnin, but first I need help" he implored, as an older man came and bent down to look Gellibrand over. This man had many pointed bone pieces piercing his skin and patterned scars across his face and chest. "My friend, Mr Hesse, he has been bitten on the face by a snake. He is waiting by a waterhole, a bit smaller than this one here. It is back up there, past those two small hills on the open plain." Gellibrand went on, looking at Murnin's face to see if she understood. "There was a kangaroo speared there, and that is where I followed footprints that led me this place" he added, thinking that

Murnin would likely know where the kangaroo had been killed by her tribesmen.

Murnin and the older man spoke for a few minutes. The older man was shaking his head and looking with contempt at Gellibrand. After this Murnin started to get up, with her string bag packed, she said, "You will come now," and she pointed towards the range of hills to the south. All the others had similarly gathered things to be ready to move.

Gellibrand remained sitting near the camp fire, "I need to eat and rest first, to regain my strength," he said, as he reclined against a rock, and took his pills from his waistcoat pocket. Before he could tip a pill out, the old man took the bottle from him, and looked inside the small hole. He looked at Gellibrand with a puzzled look, wet his finger and dipped it into the bottle. Taking a sample of the white powder, the elder put his finger in his mouth. He immediately screwed up his face and spat on the ground. He upended the contents of the bottle onto the fire before Gellibrand made a feeble attempt to snatch the bottle back.

"I needed those for my illness," Gellibrand said, looking disparaged into the fire, where the white pills burnt in strange colours of green and purple and popped with the heat. He still made no attempt to get up, even though everyone else was preparing to start walking. Murnin again spoke with the scarred man and looked at Gellibrand as the man seemed to be contemplating what to do with him.

"He wants to know why you eat poison to make yourself sick?" Murnin said, inclining her head towards the burning pills in the fire. Without waiting for an answer, she said again "You will come with us. Drink some water and come." She turned her back and moved to join the others. The elder stood menacingly over Gellibrand now.

"What about my friend?" Gellibrand asked at Murnin's now departing back.

Murnin stopped and looked back, "If the snake bit his face, he is dead already. But we will send two boys to see," she said, and again she turned and started walking.

Gellibrand thought for a moment, but he knew his only choice for survival was to stay with these savage people, no matter what the risk. He got to his feet and hurried to join the group as they filed off surprisingly swiftly towards the south-west. The men carrying two or three long spears each, with pouches of small items strung around necks or shoulders. The woman carried more possessions like the wooden bowls and small stones knives in woven baskets and string bags. There were no children with this group and all in the group were relatively young, other than the one elder who appeared to be about the same age as Gellibrand.

As they walked in single file, the elder man leading, Gellibrand and the women at the rear, Gellibrand talked with Murnin. As best she could, with her limited English skills, Murnin told him how she had been living since she was taken from the Exe River. Murnin said that she had been living around this area, at a large freshwater lake, which was one of the main camps for the people of these lands. But now the smaller clans were being gathered to move to a camp deep down in the bush on a long river, where there were plenty of fish at this time of year, to sustain a large number of people during the time that many fish moved down river and could be easily netted. She explained that for much of the year, the people lived in small groups, so that they could more easily gather enough food to feed themselves, but at certain times, like in late summer when large numbers of fish are available, all the people could gather together and feast as well as for other important matters, such as marriages and to trade goods. She explained that similar events sometimes took place on the large lakes in this area, at times when a lot of swan eggs could be collected and waterfowl hunted in large numbers.

One of the boys, Murnin pointed out, carried a stick with a row of notches cut into it. She said that these notches represented the number of days until the groups were expected to arrive at the bush camp on the river. A messenger had been sent to run around to all the small camps on the lake and the plains with the message stick. A person from each camp then copied from the message stick the number of notches remaining to the meeting day. They each then kept their message stick to mark off the days until the gathering. That way each group ended up with a stick counting down to the exact same day. These sticks were used to plan events weeks in advance, or even months by using the full moon as a fixed point in time from which to count down the days. Gellibrand asked Murnin how and when he could get back to the port town of the other white people? Murnin told him that only a few of the men, including the man who had stolen her away, would stay at the main lake to protect the camp there, so no one could be spared to take him back now. But after this gathering, when the groups dispersed across the lands again, he could go back with people from the plains close to where he had come from, who would send him back over the river to the east.

While they were walking that morning as a group, at one point they all stopped to listen to something that the old man, the one who had thrown away Gellibrand's bottle of pills, was saying to them generally while pointing to the sky ahead. Gellibrand asked Murnin what this was all about. Murnin told him, that the old man was pointing out things that he understood to mean that he was forecasting the weather for the trip down to the bush camp. For instance, Murnin told him, the old man was pointing out pairs of black cockatoos flying from the bush in the hills, out onto the open plains, and that this was a good sign that it would not rain for a few days, and that they should keep moving to get to the camp during this fine weather. Murnin explained that these things were important to watch, as storms and rain were more common in the hills and bush country, than on the open plains, and so they would keep moving quickly to get to the shelter of the river camp as soon as they were able.

Chapter eleven

The gorge was a beautiful location for a small camp for Jacky and the five surviving children. There was a small clear steam than ran all year over a rocky gravel base. Around the stream were narrow river flats that were covered in grasses and ferns save as to where the very numerous wombat holes formed excavated areas out of the grey sandy banks. The river flat was lined on both sides by very tall straight eucalypts and steep rocky hillsides that in many places formed vertical cliff faces. This made the site almost inaccessible from any direction other than walking upstream along the river in a steep gorge that stretched up into the mountain range for many many miles.

Jacky and the children had based their new camp on a grassy mound above a large pool in the river where the water wrapped almost all the way around the camp and at a point where the gorge was sufficiently wide as to allow a good deal of the sun to filter through to the floor of the gorge during the day. The opposite bank to the camp was a shear rock cliff face with just enough ledges for footholds for the children to climb a few feet above the water and then jump into the deep cool water of the main pool below.

The river gorge was teeming with birds and animals, but quite different to those of the open plains around the Exe River camp. There were wombats all along the river flats, possums in the trees, and in the evenings many of the small wallabies that lived in the forested hills above the gorge came down to the water to drink, and then to graze at night on the sweet green pick around the river.

This location would serve well to accommodate the children for a few months until the weather turned too cold to remain comfortable living in the ranges. By then Jacky will have a plan for where to take the children to be safe in the long-term. Far away from the treacherous white men who had betrayed him and his kinsmen so badly.

****

After a few months at the gorge camp, when Jacky had assessed that things would have calmed down again with the white-fellas and while the weather was still hot, he decided to make a discrete trip back to the settlement. He called the children together around a camp fire in the evening and told them that it was time he went back to see what was going on. The children were frightened. They did not want to leave the security of the rocky gorge and nor did they want Jacky to leave them alone, but he assured them he would be careful and that he would be back as soon as he was able

"I have to return to our lands to see what has become of our camp. We cannot stay in this gorge during the wet weather, it will be too cold and the river will rise to cover these grassy flats. There will be nowhere to camp, so I must go and find another safe place out on the plains."

The next morning Jacky put on his European clothes and set off at daybreak following the river that led back to the old main river camp. He did not see anyone as he made his way down stream across the plains but to be safe, he skirted along the shadows of trees and scrub as much as he could just in case anyone was watching. He did not walk through the old river camp but avoided it by cutting across the river bank so he did not have to see the site and relive such traumatic memories. But even as he skirted around the site, he could see that the area was still deserted and that no one had returned to re-establish the camp. This further confirmed his fears that the few children he had concealed in the gorge and himself were the only survivors.

As he walked, he wondered what might happen when he turned up at the settlement, but he knew there was no other way to find out what was going on in the area. He planned to keep his head down and his ears open, and at any sign of danger he was ready to flee back to the river gorge and the children who relied on him. Further down the river he found a ford from where the drays pulled by oxen had now made a well-worn path leading from the settlement to the planes out to the west. It was plain to Jacky that settlement of the area had continued unabated, or if anything the white-fella traffic had been increasing. He turned east and followed the wagon trail towards the settlement at Williamstown.

Jacky stopped under some trees before he came to the settlement and ate some cooked meat he brought with him for the trip. He was deliberately taking his time before arriving at the settlement as he thought he could slip into the town more or less unnoticed at dusk. He watched as some riders returned to town as wells as a wagon pulled by two horses, and it appeared to him that life at the settlement was going on as before.

As the sun dipped behind the rocky hills in the west, Jacky left the safety of the trees and walked quietly on the road into town. Before long he came to a camp fire where five men were sitting back drinking tea. Jacky did not recognise the men although they were not European, he spoke with them and they answered in English. One of the men gestured for him to join them by the fire and he sat down grateful for the friendly faces.

The men were dressed in European clothes and spoke English quite well and it took Jacky a while to remember how to speak in that new language. The men explained that they came from the area that the white men called Sydney town and that they came working on the ships of the white men and had been that day unloading ships at the docks in Williamstown. Jacky told them how his was the local tribe with lands just to the west of this spot and how he had had a deal with the white men to take care of the land but that this had ended badly and that he had moved his people to the hills.

Jacky was careful not to tell them too much about what happened, and he did not tell them specifically about the massacre as he did not want word to spread that might create more trouble for him and his people. At least until he could find out what was going on and to speak to Gellibrand before the other leaders of the white men found out that he was back.

Jacky slept by the fire with the other black men and in the morning with his European pants and shirt on and his hat

166

pulled low, he found that he could easily slip about the town without anyone taking any notice of him. He quickly found that the population of the town had grown considerable since he was last there. There were more huts and tents spread out across the head land and many ships at the dock and anchored nearby. He saw several white men that he recognised who were some of the original settlers, but they took no notice of him and he realised that to them he was just another black fella from the outskirts of town.

As Jacky did not know who was directly responsible for the massacre at the river camp, he thought the best place to start would be with Gellibrand but he could not see him among the white bosses around the port and he did not want to start asking questions and drawing attention to himself. Then he saw the familiar tall bushy figure of Buckley saddling up a horse near to a stable in the town. Buckley was well dressed in clothes that made him look important, but Jacky knew he was just a simple and not very intelligent man. But he thought he was one of the few men that he could trust at the settlement to fill him in on what had been going on in the past few months.

When Jacky approached Buckley, the tall white man immediately recoiled like he had seen a ghost. He looked away from Jacky and continued hitching up the girth straps on the saddle, but he spoke very quickly under his breath through his long bushy beard. He said to Jacky that he wanted nothing more to do with what was going on in the fight between the white men and the blacks. He said the white men were trying to drag him into a battle with the very people that he was trying to save. Buckley said he wanted nothing more than to leave the area and said that he had asked to be moved to Van Diemens Land just to get away from these troubles.

Jacky put his left hand on the pommel of the saddle before Buckley could mount and asked if he could just tell him where he could find Mr Gellibrand so that he could sort out a safe area for his people to camp. Buckley stood up to his full height and took a step back. "You mean to tell me you have not even heard what happened to Gellibrand?" He looked at Jacky bewildered. "It is all everybody, black and white, has been talkin' about for weeks now." He looked directly at Jacky's face but then realised that Jacky must have been out bush for some time "come here for a minute and I'll tell you what happened" Buckley whispered and took him over near a wall where they could talk privately.

Buckley told Jacky how Gellibrand and another man Hesse had gone exploring the lands to the west but had disappeared some weeks ago and had not been seen since. He told Jacky other white men, the bosses, had been trying to get Buckley to go with them to talk to the blacks in the west. But Buckley said he was scared that these white bosses were just organising more parties to go and raid the black camps and to murder more people. Buckley said that he was in trouble for refusing to help but that the Governor was agreeing to send him to Van Diemens Land so Buckley said he would take no further part in the search to find Gellibrand and Hesse.

Jacky asked Buckley why the white men could not find Gellibrand, as surely they could track two men who had been riding horses quite easily. Buckley told him how the first group who had gone searching had found that there had been a grass fire that had gone through the whole area when

168

Gellibrand and Hesse

Gellibrand and Hesse went missing. And also, how now that these searchers had been riding around on horses looking for them, it would be almost impossible after several weeks to distinguish their tracks from those of the missing men. In any case Buckley said, the white men had made up their minds that Gellibrand and Hesse had been murdered by what they called some savage tribe of blacks and so there was no point in Buckley trying to help them in the search. He told him that Gellibrand's son had been in the port town all along waiting for the return of his father and that now Gellibrand's wife had sent money and supplies to young Gellibrand to organise a large search party to go and find his father. He told Jacky to find young Gellibrand if he wanted to know what was happening with that families' lands.

Buckley mounted his horse and tipped his hat to Jacky and Jacky thanked him for his help and wished him well in Van Diemens Land, as he expected Buckley would be long gone by the time Jacky ever came to this camp again. Jacky headed into the main part of the port town where it seemed that no one was talking about the massacre on the river now, the focus appeared to be on moving stock on to the land and further developing the settlement. It did not take long for someone to tell Jacky where to find young Thomas Gellibrand and he was directed to a tent beside which were two young men.

Jacky approached the young men and asked for the young Mr Gellibrand. "I'm Thomas Gellibrand" one of the well-dressed young men replied with a curious expression on his face "and why do you want to know?" He said with a tone to his voice bordering on contempt.

"I want to help look for your father" Jacky said in a soft voice, taking his hat off his head and holding it in front of his chest. He looked at the ground before his feet.

"And why would you want to help us" he said with a scowl as he said the word 'you'. "You've heard about the reward I suppose?"

"I don't even know what that means" Jacky said looking up at the young man with a pleading face, "but I knew your father a long time and I just found out that he is gone lost. We let your father put your sheep on our land and your father take care of us."

"Oh, I see." The young man replied "but some people say that it was the deals my father made with your people that started all this trouble. Some people say that my father got your people to kill other white men like Mr Franks, who tried to bring sheep to our land. What do you say about that?"

"Me?" Jacky said, looking at the men with a puzzled expression, "don't know nought about any killin' I've been out bush a long time. I just came back to the port to find your father and now he's lost. I have to find him so then you know what he told me about our land. Your father is like my brother. I would call myself Gellibrand too if I can't find him, 'cos he good man."

Gellibrand and Hesse

Thomas Gellibrand was impressed by Jacky's story as he knew his father had befriended a local aboriginal tribe and that he had taught some of the people to speak English and he had spoken enthusiastically of employing them to work on the sheep run. He did not believe the stories that his father had instructed these men to commit murder and he too wanted his father and this man he had befriended to be able to corroborate the true story. He agreed to the offer of help and made arrangements for Jacky to be transported by ship to Geelong with other men who were forming a large expedition party to go in search of his father and the required supplies.

****

Jacky arrived by ship in the port of Geelong, on what had previously been known as Jillong Bay, he was directed to help unload supplies from the ship and take them to two waiting drays where barrels and sacks of food were loaded along with various other supplies in preparation for a long trip. Several white men were gathered nearby and were discussing plans over a makeshift map that they had laid out between them. Jacky recognised some of these white men that he had seen in the original port settlement.

At least four of the men he knew were bosses who were bringing sheep to their runs, and he recognised young Tom Armitage was with them also. There appeared to be five or six white men who were workers of these bosses and also two other black men who Jacky knew had come from Sydney. It seemed crazy to Jacky that no one from the area where Gellibrand had gone missing was going on the expedition. He

171

felt very uneasy being off his own land and in the country of other people and he could not understand how these white men operated. But he was just happy that they took no notice of him and to them he was just another black worker. The white men left the three black men together although not even understanding that they did not speak the same language and that they could only communicate because they each knew some basic English.

Once the drays were loaded up and the white men had mounted on horseback, the expedition made its way only about a mile over a large hill that formed another port settlement and down to a river where there was a rocky shallow crossing. The drays were towed by large oxen and the white men rode ahead on their horses. Jacky and the men from Sydney were just expected to walk along at the rear. Jacky wondered how long it would take to explore the lands travelling at this extremely slow pace and why the white men had to encumber themselves so many possessions for such a simple trip.

The men eventually set up a camp on the riverbank with a large camp fire where one of the men cooked a stew. The white bosses met a man there named Aikers who told them about how Gellibrand and Hesse had gone with him up the river to explore new land. Jacky listened as Aikers explained to the party how they had left the station house on the river and how Gellibrand had instructed him to take them past the area where any white man had ever been before. Aikers told them how he had tried to get Gellibrand and Hesse to return with him to the settlement area but how Gellibrand had refused insisting on exploring the land beyond.

The white bosses instructed all the men to rest for the night and that in the morning they would head off and follow the path of Gellibrand and Hesse as directed by Aikers. Neither Jacky nor any of the other men were asked to assist with tracking so they slept by the fire and in the morning filed slowly along behind the main group as before.

Again, Jacky felt very uneasy being on the country of other people, but they walked a well-worn path that roughly followed the course of the river along a wide river flat with very large hills rising from the far bank. While Jacky walked, he kept a careful observation of the landmarks around him. He wanted to be able to quickly and safely return to his own land when the time came if anything should go wrong and he lost the protection of this large party of men. The land here was very similar to that of Jacky's own land other than the large rolling hills that went away to the south, but he could see that this land had been grazed by sheep as was no longer in its natural state.

The large group continued to make very slow progress along the wagon trail until about midday when they came to a large house built on a bend in the river. Here the party stopped and the bosses went to the house where apparently they sat down for lunch with the owner while Jacky and the other workers made a fire by the river to cook their own lunch. The white men made it clear that Jacky was to be with the other black men, and the men from Sydney were used to cooking white man's food so they welcomed Jacky to their fire and made sure that he ate well with them. Jacky was content to sit back and not draw attention to himself and in any case, he seemed invisible to the white bosses and that

173

suited him fine for now.

By the end of this first day Aikers had led the expedition to the junction in the river where he says that Gellibrand insisted on deviating from where Aikers was supposed to be guiding him to the next station house, to instead explore the other side of the river. Aikers explained where he had gone with Gellibrand and Hesse further south along the branch of the river and from where he had eventually turned back. The white bosses decided that this would be the place to set up base camp and from here a smaller expedition party would strike out to cover a much larger area in search of the missing men. The oxen were released from their harness and the horses hobbled while Jacky and the other workmen went about setting up the camp.

Jacky could see from here the land as Aikers had described it. Before them, towards the low setting sun he could see a broad plain stretching out that was completely black from a recent grass fire that appeared to have swept through as far as the eye could see. About here the large hills ended and now to the South was also a broad river flat although another range of hills could be seen at a great distance on the horizon. Jacky guessed that the fire had been started by lightning because there would be no need for the local people to burn the grass in the hot season. And he knew there was only two causes of fire and that was by lightening or by man. If the locals were to burn the grass, they would do it just before the rains came at the end of the hot season so that the resulting new green grass would attract more kangaroos and emus to the area for hunting later on. They would not start a fire in the heat and wind when the fire would spread wild and fast and just create danger.

The white bosses sat around the camp fire that night and made a plan to do a broad sweep of the area over the next few days. Jacky listened on as they talked about riding as far south as they could go to the distant hills and then sweeping around to the West in an attempt to cross the tracks of the missing men. About half the men would stay at the base camp and the other half would go in the search party with just enough supplies for a few days but with enough guns and ammunition to defend themselves should they need to. Jacky heard one of the white bosses saying that a black man had come to them in Geelong, claiming that he knew that Gellibrand and Hesse had been murdered at a big lake that is located to the west along the foothills of the distant ranges. It was the plan of this search party to eventually come to that lake, to see if they were able to find the tracks of the missing men and to investigate this claim further.

Again, that night Jacky and the men from Sydney cooked and slept beside their own fire on the riverbank while the white men occupied the main camp.

The next morning the white bosses prepared their horses, loading them with blankets, guns and supplies with the search party ready to leave the base camp and begin the search proper. They asked Jacky and the two other black men to come with them on foot and to scout the ground as they went for any sign or tracks of the missing men. All the rest of the men stayed behind to take care of the base camp while the search party would be away. Jacky was pleased to finally have a task to occupy his time and to use his skills, as the progress thus far had been excruciatingly slow compared with how

Jacky would normally travel. He could still not understand why white men had to travel with so much stuff and stop so often for such things as cups of tea.

Jacky now took the lead of this search party as he darted along by foot following the small river in a roughly southerly direction and scanning about for signs of the missing men. The two Sydney men also fanned out on foot and five men on horseback walked their steeds slowly along.

The mounted men's broad-brimmed hats shadowed their faces and they frequently shooed flies from their eyes. These men did not speak much, but they were constantly watching the terrain ahead and also the horizon to the west. An unspoken tension hung in the air caused by the risk of attack from the legendary hostile inhabitants which would most likely come from the west, or an ambush along the river.

After a while Jacky found a shallow sandy part of the river where he could see that someone had crossed with at least two horses. He pointed this out to the bosses but said that he did not know if this was from Gellibrand and his friend, or someone looking for him since. The tracks were not that fresh as he could see that rain had fallen and distorted the prints in the soft earth since they had been made. In any case, the white men conferred and decided that they needed to cross the river to continue south toward the ranges, so they may as well cross here and try to follow the path previously made by whomever had crossed.

Once over the river, Jacky felt even more uneasy than he had before. This river was the most distant border that anyone from his people should cross, uninvited, and he was now without a doubt committing a serious trespass on the country of other peoples. He was now beyond the point of no return and may now suffer whatever consequences this trespass may bring. Now that his world had been turned upside down and his wife and family gone, he felt he had nothing left to lose and, prior to the appearance of the white man in his land, he never would have even contemplated such a brazen affront on his neighbours' rights.

Just as Jacky was deep in thought about what horrible fate might befall him for his breach, one of the white men called halt. There were black men approaching. Jacky quickly squatted in the grass, with the rest of the party behind him, he scanned ahead and around to the west, but he could not see anybody. He slowly swivelled right around on the balls of his feet and then he saw that the white men had half-turned their horses. The white men were all watching men coming up from the river, unexpectedly from the same place where this party had just crossed.

The approaching men were a mob of about ten young black men, with thick white and orange lines painted over their dark skin and feathers and other bushy decorations around their wrists, ankles and heads. They each carried more than one long spear in the usual vertical position and the white paint in circles around the eyes and lines across the foreheads made them look particularly menacing. They jogged along at a quick pace in a jaunty but tight bunch.

Some of the white men put their hands around the pistol grip of their weapons and a hammer was drawn back with that familiar metal 'click'. Jacky however could see that, although the young men looked prepared for war, they were ambling along and chattering and not preparing to attack at all. Before

177

the white men could react further Jacky walked quickly back between them and the approaching party and put his palms up and said to the mounted white men "It is alright! These men are my men and not going to hurt you." He walked backwards facing the white men with his hands still raised in a conciliatory gesture until he was almost standing with the band of young black men before any of the white bosses could react.

The white bosses sat up in the saddles of the horses scratching their heads and looking at each other, wondering why these men were walking up from the way they had come and in the middle of nowhere. They had not come from the west, as they had expected an approach may come and this confused them.

While these young fellows were not exactly his men, these men were from the same language group as Jacky and part of his broader community. They were definitely not men from the west of the river. Jacky spoke with them and found out that they were men from the Barrabool Hills, the long range of hills along which Jacky and the search party had walked the past day and half before passing the end of the hills and turning south along this river branch. Jacky quickly ascertained who these men knew and found that sure enough, some of these young men were his cousins and certainly not a danger to him and this search party. They looked up to Jacky as an elder of their community and keeper of their traditional lands and greeted him warmly and with great respect.

"What are you men doing here? Where are you going dressed for war", Jacky asked them in the local language. Looking the men up and down and gesturing to the long spears carried by the warriors.

"We heard about the search party going into the Lake Country, and we are not missing the opportunity." said the apparent leader of these men, with a big grin on his face.

"This is not funny, and it is not your problem." Jacky said, scowling at the young man. "I have to break custom and go into this land, you men do not."

"Ha ha, but we do," the young man retorted, his eyes wide open and intense, "The Lake Country people steal our women for wives. Not long ago, another young girl was snatched by a Lake Country man sneaking across our hills and fleeing back across this river." He held his head high, no longer smiling at Jacky. "We will seek revenge for our people if we are with you or not. We will get our girl, or one of theirs, and spear the man in the leg who took her. You know the law Jacky. If he lives, he lives, if he dies from the wound then it was meant to be. That is fair punishment."

One of the white bosses became impatient and called out to Jacky asking what was going on. Jacky told him that these men were on a trip that had nothing to do with their expedition and were just passing through. Jacky walked a short distance from the search party with his arm around the shoulder of the young leader of the group as the other young warriors followed close behind. Jacky whispered close to the young man's ear. He looked at Jacky, smiled, and then lead his war party off continuing in a direction due west from the river out across the open plains.

"Come on then!" Jacky called to the rest of his expedition party, as he jogged theatrically ahead of them, urging them to continue the search along the river to the south-west, and hurrying on before the white men asked any more questions. The white bosses just looked at each other, shrugged, and then kicked their horses back up to a walking pace. The small band of warriors quickly disappeared as they marched over the rise to the west without looking back at the search party that plodded slowly along.

The search party made very slow progress as the group zigzagged around the hard open ground looking for tracks or any sign of the missing explorers. As the search party came close to the foothills of the ranges they swept around to the west as planned. By the time they reached another small dry creek and then a small round lake, teaming with water-fowl, it was time to start making a camp for the evening. Once again, the white men looked after themselves and ignored the black men.

Jacky used this time to walk ahead to a rocky outcrop on the next hill that would make a good vantage point from which to scan the view to the west and plan the search for the following day. Before he reached the hill, Jacky could see that this had been the site of a very recent camp by the arrangement of rocks and wood near a blackened camp fire pit. Jacky walked very carefully and deliberately through the camp scanning the ground for signs. And there he found something remarkable. The clear heel-print from someone wearing a shoe, a print made some time ago, but still preserved in the soft black ash area beside what had been a camp fire.

When Jacky returned to the camp, he told young Mr Armitage that he had found the track of a white man in the camp on the hill, and that it was not likely made by the other search party as they had not found the hoof marks of any horses near here. That night there was a buzz going through the camp in anticipation of what the search party would find the next day when it arrived in the heart of the Lake Country people.

Jacky had a particularly disturbed sleep that night. He kept having vivid dreams, including one where the sun rose in the east in the morning, and the sun spoke to him in a woman's voice, calling him back to his people and to abandon his journey into foreign lands. But while Jacky stood contemplating what the sun was saying to him, a huge eagle flew circling between him and the sun. This eagle was so large it was blocking out the sun so that Jacky could no longer see the sun, nor hear what it called to him. During this eclipse several falcons swiftly swooped down about his head and each spoke whispered words to him in his native language as they whooshed past his ears.

"kill"

"Revenge"

"Mongrel dogs"

"Thieves"

"kill the white dogs"

****

In the morning, after Jacky showed the white bosses the footprint in the ashes, the party headed off early and with renewed energy. Jacky and the other trackers quickly found the trail where the party of people from the camp had travelled away to the west. It appeared to Jacky from the tracks that at least one white man was travelling with a group of the local tribe away on foot from this camp. Presumably, the search party leaders surmised, taken hostage.

The trail followed the contours of the foothills with the steeper ranges and bush to the left, and the vast plains stretching out to the right. It was not long before the trail dropped down over the crest of the first line of hills to a small creek and continued downstream along this pretty little creek, with scattered old gum trees along the bank, and the pools of water teeming with waterfowl. Jacky noticed the familiar scar on a large tree where a sheet of bark had been cut out in the shape used to form a canoe, so he knew that the creek must form a larger body of water further downstream.

After only a couple of hours going at walking pace, Jacky gestured to the group to stop, and he spotted far ahead tendrils of smoke trailing out from the canopy of the stand of gum trees further up the creek flat. The men dismounted from the horses and rested for a short time. This time Jacky insisted that they not make tea lest the smoke from the fire would alert anyone to their presence. The group readily agreed and instead the men drank from the water bags that hung from the saddles and ate biscuits made of oatmeal.

Jacky squatted on his haunches and spoke to the white men who were gathered in the shade of one large gum tree.

"You know that Buckley refused to come on this search because the white men on the first search fucked it up by not letting him speak with the local people first. I know this 'cos he told me his self."

The white men frowned and exchanged glances at the tone of the language Jacky used to speak with them, but they let him go on, and no one challenged the fact of what he stated.

"There are people camped ahead where that fire is, and they are not going to be happy with strangers walking on their country. Especially white men and strange black fellas all armed with guns and spears. You have to let me go in first and speak with them in a shared language, and with signs that you are not here to fight, but to find your missing friends. If we give respect and tell them that we will leave them in peace they might help us."

Jacky looked around the group with a stern look on his face, and the white men met his gaze, but none spoke or questioned the logic of what he suggested. When his eyes met those of Mr Armitage, the young white man tipped his head just enough to acknowledge that he consented, so Jacky rose and walked on.

The party walked on up the valley that spread out before them and they could see that the stand of gum trees marked the point where the creek flowed into a large lake beyond the trees. As they walked up the valley the lake appeared to be very large, as they could not see the east or west edges of the lake for the hills on either side of the creek, but the prominent hills visible on the northern shore were a faint blue-grey against the horizon and it was obviously many miles across. The party continued at a slow walking pace, quietly moving and no one spoke. As the party got closer to the lake the creek flooded out over more of the flat ground, and they walked around the right-hand bank and from there followed a well-worn foot trail down toward what must be a camp in the stand of gum trees just ahead.

As the party approached the bush at the mouth of the creek, where it met the shoreline of the lake, they could not see far as wattle scrub and tea-tree grew between the tall gum trees and along the shallows of the lake very tall reeds covered many acres of land. Jacky could feel the hairs on the back of his neck stand up as he walked about 50 yards ahead of the others towards where the smoke rose from a camp fire. He knew that the inhabitants would have to hear the horses soon, snorting and rattling the bridles they wore, but he had no idea how many people would be there, and how they were going to react to seeing this party. They might never have seen white men on horses with guns before, and they would no doubt be angry that he too was on their land.

Just as these thoughts went through his mind, a tall dark figure walked boldly forward, out of the bush to meet with Jacky, only about 20 yards away. Behind and on both sides of this figure were other faces appearing slowly out of the shadows of what appeared to be a few children and at least one old man. Jacky's mouth fell open at the surprise when he saw the face of the man, with his chin held high. It was none other than Tanapia himself.

Tanapia was unarmed and Jacky had left his spears with one of the Sydney men to carry, so he approached Tanapia with his arms held out at each side, carrying only his waddie in his right hand as always. Tanapia stood arrogantly waiting with his arms folded across his chest for Jacky to walk up to him. The other faces of the onlookers held back in the shadows, and Jacky put his open left hand up in the air without looking back, as the sign for the search party to stop and wait where they were, which they did.

When Jacky walked up to meet Tanapia, he opened his mouth to speak the speech he had rehearsed in his head many times in the last couple of days, about how the party had trespassed on the land only to find the missing important white men and to leave again as soon as they could. But the shock of being met there by Tanapia, and the strange smug look that was on that man's face had confounded him.

In any case, Tanapia spoke first.

"You are too late Jacky, go home."

"What do you mean too late?" Jacky responded, "Do you know what happened to them?"

"She has already gone away, to be married, so go home now, and take these men with you."

"Murnin? You have Murnin? And you are getting married?" Jacky was really astonished now, and his head was spinning with the thought that she was still alive. This changed everything. He needed a new plan, and quickly.

"No." Tanapia said, chuckling, "I don't want and old frog like her for my wife. She was a present for my uncle, a great man of the south."

Before Tanapia knew what hit him, Jacky had thrust the sharp end of his waddy up and straight into the heart and lung area, puncturing the skin just below Tanapia's ribs. Jacky held the waddy vertically, His right hand firmly on the shaft, his left hand holding the ball of the club at the base, with Tanapia impaled to a depth of about 8 inches. Jacky and Tanapia's faces were almost touching, but now Tanapia did not look smug, his eyes rolled back, and for a few moments all that held him upright was the force of the weapon, warm blood gushing down and over Jacky's hands as the life quickly drained from the big man's body. Jacky took one step back, withdrawing the shaft swiftly from the chest cavity, and let Tanapia's dead body slump to the ground.

There were loud gasps and then the pattering sound of small running footsteps in the bush, and then from behind him the thunderous sound of horse's hooves cantering up to the scene where Jacky stood over the body of the Lake Country man. Jacky looked up, young Mr Armitage looked furious.

"What the hell did you do that for? Is this how you get cooperation with the local savages is it?"

Jacky looked calmly up at the white man on horseback.

"He killed Gellibrand and Hesse. Him and his people. They killed them and threw them into the lake right here. Down there in the water in that tall grass."

As the men on the horses looked at each other, and down through the bush at the reeds on the edge of the lake, they were again caught by surprise by the same band of young warriors who had passed them back near the Barrabool Hills. The young men still wore the feathers and body paint and they ran up from behind the search party, calling out in high pitched yelps of excitement. Before the men of the search party could react, the warriors over took them, and ran into the bush pursuing the locals who had fled from the incident.

The children and old men had run back into the main camp area and then into the tall reeds beside the lake that were taller than an average man. This was one of the main camps of the Lake Country people and would normally be home to a large number of family groups at any one time. However, as the large gathering had been arranged at the river camp, almost everybody had left the lake and was travelling down the valley to the river area. The few people left in the camp had stayed behind to maintain the camp and to meet up with other relatives coming through to travel together to the celebrations in the last few days before the full moon.

Tanapia and a few old men had stayed behind to guard this strip of lake frontage, that was one of the most valued pieces of land held onto by their people. This large freshwater lake was a great source of food and fresh water to the people, as most of the other lakes around the area were salty, or too small to hold water all year round. Over hundreds of years, and many hard-fought battles, most of the larger family groups of the Lake Country people had each secured their own strip of lake frontage land. As this particular place had not only lake frontage, but a running creek and bush cover, Tanapia and many others believed that this was the most highly prized camp in the whole of the land. While it had been land held by his ancestors for generations now, Tanapia would not leave the camp unattended for all but the briefest period for the big celebration at the river camp and had planned to only go down the valley for the main night on the full moon.

After only a few chaotic minutes, while the white men had only had time to exchange glances and wonder what on earth was going on about them, the band of young warriors emerged again from the cover of the bush. This time they were all smiling and laughing among themselves, and had their long spears casually resting on their shoulders or used them as walking sticks as they strode triumphantly back to the spot where the local man lay dead on the ground. The reason that they now appeared triumphant, was that the leader of the group now carried under his arm, like he might carry a rag doll, a young naked girl of about ten or eleven years of age. She struggled and kicked with her legs and pulled at the young warriors arm with hers in an attempt to get her face close enough to bite him. The young warrior was far too strong to worry about her protestations and he held her tight as the group stopped near the body of the dead elder.

Before the men of the search party had time to comprehend what was happening, one of the young warriors rolled the dead body of the man over so that he lay face down, in the large pool of his own blood. He then quickly and expertly made an incision with a sharp tool, that fitted very neatly between his thumb and forefinger, down each side of the man's back, just below his ribs. Little blood came from the cuts now that the body had bled out and had laid there for a while, and the man shoved his right hand into one of the incisions, and then quickly pulled it free holding a kidney in his fist, while cutting with the sharp tool the connecting tissues, being careful to retain the thick layer of fat attached at one end of the kidney. He dropped that kidney on the man's bare back while he quickly repeated the operation on the other side before holding the pair of organs above his head laughing, to the cheers and laughter of the other young warriors, who all began to walk off back towards their home lands, up the hill to the east. The white men each turned on their horses in horrified disbelief at what was happening and watched slack-jawed as the young men marched away. One of the men called after them.

"What are you doing? Where are you taking them?"

The leader of the young warriors turned, with the struggling girl still securely under his right arm, with the most serious expression on his faced called back in English. "We are going to eat them, of course." And with that he and the other young men turned and walked on laughing and joking as they disappeared back over the hill and left the search party staring after their brightly painted backs.

The white bosses huddled back together, they had to take back charge of the situation and continue with their mission to find the lost explorers. They decided that they would ride into the camp on the horses, making a lot of noise and firing guns to scare off the remaining locals. They would then conduct a systematic search of the area, particularly of the shallow waters and the reeds where the now deceased man had indicated that the bodies had been thrown. They decided that if any other witness was found, Jacky was not to harm them and was to speak with the prisoner only under the supervision of one of the leaders.

When the men broke from this impromptu meeting they looked about for Jacky, but he could not be found. The two black men from Sydney squatted under the shade of a small wattle waiting and watching. When one of the white men asked where Jacky was, they both shrugged, with blank expressions on their faces. They waited for direction on what to do next.

These two men knew that searching the shallows was a waste of time, but they also knew that no one would listen to their opinion about that, so they just waited and said nothing. They recognised that this was indeed a prime camp site, with an abundance of resources and clean fresh water. There was no way on earth that the custodians of this land would pollute their main water source with the bodies of dead men. If anything, the local people would have put the bodies in a tree far from the water and let them decay where they could do no harm to the state of this pristine environment.

In any case, the search party went on plundering the camp site. They scared off the owners and systematically conducted an unproductive search of a large area of the tall reed beds in the shallows of the lake.

Nearby, Jacky had tracked one of the fleeing old men into a large stand of tall reeds a couple of hundred yards west of the main camp, in a small shallow bay. He captured and pinned the old man by the shoulders on the muddy ground, with his large hunting knife held across the throat of the old man. The old man was shaking his head, with his eyes closed in defiance, but Jacky then slowly pressed the knife harder against the side of the old man's neck, where the main artery runs.

Chapter twelve

Jogging through the sparse forest, Jacky made quick time now that he was free of the plodding band of white men. He was also free of the long spears that he had left another man holding during the brief clash with Tanapia, and only had the hunting knife at the back of his belt and his waddie still in his possession. The old man had eventually disclosed the location of the river camp and so escaped with his life. He had drawn a rough map with his finger in the mud, showing that there was another valley to the south west. Not the small valley that they had followed along the creek to get to the camp, but a large valley that eventually formed into a river that ran south to the open sea. Jacky just to had run south west over the range until he cut any small river or creek running south. This would then lead him to the main river and then he would have to come inevitably to the river camp. It was a two day walk, the old man had said, but Jacky knew he could make quick time travelling alone, and also that he would soon find tracks of other people heading to the river camp that he could follow and save the time of trying to navigate along the main river himself.

At the river camp, people had arrived in dribs-and-drabs over recent days. The main camp was in a clump of gum trees on the east bank of the river where it formed a large pool of brown foamy water. At this time of year, the river was a series of large deep pools, with shallower narrow runs in between, where in places a person could even wade across to the other side. The camp was at a point where the valley opened up from a narrow rocky gorge into a broad river flat, particularly wide on the east side of the river, but on the west side, almost vertical black rocky cliffs formed below tall hills covered in thick bush.

As people arrived, they paid respects to the elders of the river camp country, and then moved on to the flats just to the south and set up smaller camp sites of their own. In between the main camp of the owners of the land, and the flats where smaller camps popped up, a large ceremonial field had been prepared. This field consisted of a large round area clear of trees and bordered by large rocks and logs that were around the perimeter of the circle and used for the men to sit on during the ceremonies. The women would have their own ceremonies, held separately and away from the men. It was still three days until the main events that would take place on the night of the full moon, with marriage ceremonies to be conducted the following morning.

Murnin had continued to be entrusted with the task of caring for Gellibrand. Otherwise she just waited forlornly at the main river camp for her marriage to the older man in a few short days. As she was from foreign lands, and Gellibrand was a complete stranger to this river and ranges country, the two aliens had formed an unlikely bond in the circumstances.

Murnin had now met the elder with whom she was to be wedded. He was a greatly respected elder who already had two other wives. The elder told Murnin how his family group moved between camps on their lands but how he favoured living close to the mouth of this river where it meets the sea. There, he told her, he had a whole village of huts with stone foundations and large shady roofs, and there they would have access to the best foods that the open seas could provide. Murnin was very sad however and thought constantly about Jacky and longed to be back with her own people on the river plains of her own country. She also worried herself almost sick about what had become of her people, she thought about who might have survived the bloody massacre and what had become of her real husband.

Gellibrand had been driving Murnin almost mad with his incessant talking. He had regained his strength and again had the vigour of a younger man. Since disposing of his toxic medications and being on a diet of bush herbs, prescribed for him by the same old man who disposed of his white pills, and good food Gellibrand was in better health than he had been for some years. His renewed energy and recent experiences had him talking endlessly about his new ambitions to help the native peoples of this land, to manage the land cooperatively with them, and not to see them be oppressed by other white settlers.

He preached about forming alliances with the elders, with creating large reserves of land for the exclusive use of the local people. And not just reserves on the fringes of the good farming land, but large reserves of land in prime positions, in each family or language group's country. He had the influence with the settlers, and the connections through his networks to make this happen he said. This he promised to Murnin as he paced about beside the camp fire one day, hands clasped behind his back, speaking up to the sky and the trees, while Murnin nodded, and pretended to believe what he said. As the only person in the camp who understood some English, she knew that she was stuck with the job of listening to his apparently heart-felt aspirations, at least for the next few days anyway.

Gellibrand had, even in these primitive surroundings, sought to maintain the airs and graces of an English gentleman. He regularly brushed off and maintained his coat as best he could and cleaned his now tattered buckle-up boots. He proudly wore a gold watch and fob chain on his waistcoat and always had his two pistols worn decoratively in his belt. Gellibrand had not yet told Murnin of his plans, but Gellibrand thought he may even be able to give a key note address to these people on the night of the main ceremony, with Murnin as his interpreter, to tell these people how to best protect their title to the land and other legal rights that they should seek to assert under the laws of England to which they would all soon be subjected. They just had to return him safely to the settlement at Geelong, and he would promise to be a life-long advocate for the natives.

By dusk, Jacky had reached a high point in the ranges. The bush changed as he moved further south, and the hills became higher and the valley below much deeper. The bush on the ranges was made up of low tea-tree scrub and scattered rough brown gum trees, where he saw the odd kangaroo and many small lizards. On this high point, and on the steep slopes before him, magnificent tall gums trees grew with hard smooth white trunks and the spread of the branches and leaves formed a canopy high above. The ground was getting soft and damp with many green ferns growing in the layer of fallen leaves and rotting bark below the tall timber. He had flushed several small black wallabies as he jogged along similar to those that lived near his camp in the gorge on his own country. The birds here were also similar to those of his gorge country, with small flocks of rosellas often announcing his approach with loud screeches of alarm as they alighted from the trees above. The hills and small valleys before him sloped off to the south and from this very high vantage point, he could see for a long way over a very large valley running away roughly to the south. At the extreme southern horizon, he could just make out another ridge of large hills that gave the appearance that these ranges went on for a great distance before the river dropped into the sea somewhere beyond sight as the old man had described to him.

At a distance of probably a few hours walk, Jacky could see a few columns of smoke rising out from the cover of the gum trees right at the floor of the main valley below. He knew that this would be the camps of the people gathering for the ceremony on the river. He had been following a route marked by the passage of other recent foot traffic so Jacky went east a few hundred yards to find a place to camp on this ridge for the night, away from the likely path of other travellers, and also to evade anyone who may have been deliberately following his tracks.

The next morning, the local people were busy in the main river camp, preparing for the arrival of more visitors for the ceremonies fast approaching. Many young men were gathering for a hunting party and were armed with several long spears each. The women were mainly sorting and repairing some long woven eel traps that they then took down to the river to set on the shallow rocky river runs. As well as catching the eels that were on the move in this river, particularly at night and in the early morning, the children were encouraged to swim in the large pools above the runs to scare any fish that might then be flushed into the nets as well.

Jacky had been on the move that morning since before sunrise. He had memorised the geography of the land he looked over the night before, as he knew that once he dropped down into the bush, he would not be able to see far ahead to keep a straight course. He had picked out several high peaks and cliffs as markers for plotting his journey as he made his way closer to where he had seen the smoke of the camp fires. He followed a small creek that ran downhill to the south-west, and soon found that it joined with a larger river at the bottom of the valley and that ran more to the south. This river was more of a brown and muddy colour than his river at home. It contained less sand and rock than he expected, but he soon found a large gum tree fallen right across the river where he was able to cross without having to wade the muddy bed.

Jacky knew that the obvious and easy course to the river camp was by continuing to follow the river flat on the east side, as the trail he had been walking on seemed to be going. But he wanted to skirt along the western side of the river, by traversing along above the black rocky cliffs where he was far less likely to encounter any other people. He could not just walk into the camp unannounced and he could not know whether or not a runner might have escaped the lake camp after he despatched Tanapia and taken news to this camp of his apparent treachery.

As expected, when Jacky moved along the ridge on the western side of the river, after some considerable and skilful climbing, he eventually came to a point where he was looking down from quite a height into the main river camp below. He set himself up for a long period of surveillance, by settling down between some large rocks. There was also some low scrub from which he could watch the camp, and his position was well concealed from the casual gaze of the people passing way below. He was pleased to see that most, if not all the men, had departed the camp in a hunting party and that the women had moved down the river to where there were narrow runs, and that the children had gone with them. He had not seen his wife in the group of women who moved out of the main camp and he did not know what to make of this. All he could do for the mean time was watch and wait.

After some time, the sun rose high enough above the big hills to shine morning sunlight directly onto the rocks around the river below his position and adjacent to the main camp. Something moving below the trees in that area caught Jacky's attention. He audibly gasped as he saw his beautiful wife Murnin walk out onto a large flat rock on the western side of the river, with none other than Mr J T Gellibrand himself.

****

In the depths of the valley it was still quite cool in the shade of the tall gums that surrounded the main river camp. Gellibrand had his coat on, but Murnin had nothing but the rug under which she had slept to keep her warm. She noticed that the rising sun was shining brightly on the large flat rock ledge on the opposite side of the river from where they sat. Everyone else had left the camp site early that morning, getting ready for the approaching ceremonies, and once again Murnin was left behind to babysit Gellibrand.

Murnin got up and gestured for Gellibrand to follow her down to the river. Murnin let the rug fall off her shoulders to the ground and she walked slowly down to a large pool that had a reasonably clean grey-sandy bank where people had frequently bathed. She squatted down at the water's edge and splashed the cool water on her face and let the water run over her shoulders and chest, sending a shiver through her body and Gellibrand noticed the goose bumps that appeared down the back of her arms. Murnin then walked along to the head of the pool where a large fallen tree made a natural bridge across the shallow run of water and Gellibrand followed as she skipped nimbly across the log.

On the broad rock ledge Murnin sat down facing the sun. She closed her eyes and relaxed back against the now warming wall of smooth black rock. Gellibrand also sat in the sun and leaned against a large rock. He had not slept very well by the camp fire the night before and was still sleepy. He thought he might lay back and get a bit more sleep in the warm morning sun. With his head back and his arm shading his eyes, he could not help but study the beautiful face and body of the young women stretched out before him. Droplets of glistening water still fell from her hair and face onto her bare breasts where the cool water made her skin visible prickle.

He could see why this attractive and intelligent young woman was a sought-after prize for the local elder who was about to marry her. He now felt a warm affection for Murnin and was feeling sorry for her, for being taken from her family and friends and stolen away to new lands and married off by force. He thought about this as he closed his eyes and dozed. He thought about what he could do to advocate for the rights of these native inhabitants of the land and also what he might do in the future to help Murnin especially. He felt particularly responsible for the situation in which he had found her, given his involvement with her clan and the subsequent massacre that had happened while he was back in Van Diemens Land. He assumed that there was no family for her to return to in her home lands, so he could not think what he could do to help her in any case. He knew that it was only a couple of days now until the ceremonies would be complete, and he could leave with the group from the north to make his way back to civilisation. It was more than likely he would never see Murnin again.

Jacky climbed down the escarpment from where he had been spying over the main camp and then he crept slowly along the river bank, moving with the deliberate silence of a well-practised and skilful hunter. He was forced to the eastern bank by the steep rocks and had to cross the river where he could use the cover of the shadows and the thick ferns to conceal his approach. He knew from his observations since sunrise that most of the people were away or further downstream, but as the consequence for being discovered sneaking into the camp was almost certainly death, he did not take any unnecessary chances.

Just as these thoughts were going through his mind, Jacky heard the crackle of dry twigs over his left shoulder. He quickly ducked down below the level of the tops of the ferns and held his breath. When he carefully peered through the foliage in the direction of the sounds, he saw a couple of kids, probably in their early teens, holding hands and giggling silently each with their free hand over their own mouth. The couple looked back towards the camp, apparently to see if anyone was following them, and then they went sneaking off together up the trail to the north, giggling sheepishly, the girl leading the boy quickly along as they disappeared over the rise and into the bush beyond.

Jacky sat completely motionless in the undergrowth for a good couple of minutes, making sure that no one else was around. He could feel his heart beating in his chest so hard that he wondered for a moment if that would not give away his concealment. Once he had become sure that he was safe, and he had controlled his breathing into even and quiet repetitions, he continued downstream. When he came to a very large log across the river, where a tree had fallen some years ago, he crept forward along the shadows in a crouch using that log as cover. He leaned his back against the log, knowing that he must now be getting close to the main camp area, sitting silently again for a good couple of minutes, listening for any sign of people being in the area.

Feeling slowly around at the back of his trousers, Jacky located the hunting knife in the sheath hanging there on his belt. He wrapped his hand around the hard leather handle and slid the blade out carefully. He also moved his hand down the handle of his waddie so that if he needed to, he was ready to swing that implement like a club. Once he revealed himself to Murnin, he had no way of knowing who, or how many people might appear and try to stop their escape, so he had to be ready to strike quickly and effectively if they were going to make it safely away from the camp.

Jacky raised himself and turned around to peer carefully over the top of the large log, that was almost as high as he was tall. He saw that beyond the log was a large pool in the river, with tall gums to his left, and a rocky bank on the right. His heart again began to quicken as Jacky realised that he was very close to the location where he had hoped to emerge, near the rocky ledge where he had seen his Murnin.

Slowly Jacky moved to his right, stepping slowly and silently into the shallow water, staring into the shadows where the main camp must be located under the tall trees. When he could not detect any movement in the camp, he continued to move across the river and to focus his attention on the other side. Of course, it would have been easier to cross the river by walking along the top of the log, but this would make him highly visible and would be far too risky. He could see a black rock bank on the far side, with a high cliff behind. The cliff was almost vertical, with many horizontal ledges and lines running through the formation. In some of these fissures, tufts of grass and small wattle shrubs jutted out of the otherwise blank wall of rock. As he moved closer to the rock ledge and he felt with his feet for the muddy bank, he could see further onto the platform formed by the rock, and against the far wall he saw Murnin and Gellibrand both sitting in the sun. Gellibrand looked to be dozing, with his head back and his eyes closed, and Murnin sat with her legs crossed and was busy focussed on doing something with her hands, perhaps weaving a small basket out of the reeds, he thought.

Jacky now came to the point where the log met the rock, and the top of the log was about level with the surface of the rock platform. He looked back over his shoulder, continually checking that no one was watching from the main camp area. As he watched back that way, he swung his legs up slowly and quietly, so that he was lying flat on the top of the log. As he turned back towards Gellibrand, he started to crawl forward, he moved on his elbows, as he held a weapon in each hand, and focussed on Gellibrand, like a hunter stalking his prey. As he moved his elbows forward a quick movement caught his eye in the foreground. A large blue-tongue skink had been sunning itself on the rock right in front of him, but due to its dark cobalt blue and grey colour, he had not seen it until it moved.

The large lizard quickly spun in a 180-degree arc to face-down Jacky. It opened its mouth wide and hissed loudly in a move of defensive bravado. Jacky was not sure if it was this sound, or if he involuntarily gasped himself, but at that instant Gellibrand sat straight up with a startled expression, and looked straight into the face of Jacky, creeping on his elbows from the river, with a weapon in each hand. Jacky froze for an instant, and with a flick of its tail the lizard disappeared off the rock and down a crevice somewhere.

"Jacky, you are alive!" Murnin cried as she heard the sound too and looked at Jacky.

Jacky looked at Murnin and signalled with his hand to his mouth for her to be quiet. His eyes pleading with her, and she understood immediately, that he did not want to alert people to his presence.

Before Jacky could move from the prone position on the log, Gellibrand had sprung to his feet and began to scramble up the rock wall that he had been resting against. The horizontal cracks and crevices made for a natural ladder, and even one who was as bad a bushman as Gellibrand, could ascend the rock wall very quickly. Gellibrand climbed as a man fleeing for his life would and muttered to himself under his panicked breath. He kept saying things about how he had not caused the death of Jacky's tribe, and how all he would do now is help the native people.

Murnin ran to embrace Jacky as he jumped up and stood on the rock ledge, looking up at Gellibrand climbing to a height very swiftly. He pressed Murnin's face to his chest briefly, but he looked from Gellibrand to the main camp, fearing that soon Gellibrand scurrying about on the rock wall would draw attention from people as he would be visible from very far away. Clambering awkwardly up, in his fancy English clothes and his silly buckled shoes. Jacky threw down his waddie and slipped the knife back into the sheath on his belt. He gently moved Murnin aside and ran quickly to the rock wall to pursue the fleeing Englishman.

As Gellibrand ascended the cliff his eyes bulged with fear as he was sure that Jacky had mysteriously appeared from the bush with intent to murder him. Gellibrand had been so

203

affected by the massacre of the tribe on his land that the only thought that came to his mind when he saw Jacky creeping up armed with weapons was that he had hunted Gellibrand down to seek retribution for his people. He continued to climb higher and higher, desperate with fear and muttering incoherently. He soon heard the sounds of Jacky climbing swiftly up the cliff below him and he knew that he could not escape capture by the experienced bushman. Yet Gellibrand continued to climb, as tears began to stream down his face. But he lost his momentum, and struggled to move hand over hand, from crevice to crevice, looking no further forward through tearful eyes than each hand hold he could squeeze his fingertips into.

Soon Gellibrand reached the ledge at the top of the rock wall where the ground levelled off somewhat and the tall bush and scrub grew. As he put his hands up to feel the ledge above him, he looked back over his shoulder at the man below. Jacky focused deliberately on finding each secure hand and foot hold as he climbed steadily up only about half way up the 30-foot rock face. It flashed through Gellibrand's mind that he had a chance now to run into the bush, and perhaps Jacky would not follow but return to his wife to escape this area himself with her, and Gellibrand thought he might yet go free.

As this desperate hope flashed through his mind Gellibrand turned back to the task of climbing up onto the rock ledge and getting into the cover of the scrub beyond. He heaved himself up with both hands so that his head and shoulders came awkwardly up above the ridge that formed the cliff top. As he looked forward to see what he might be able to grab hold of, to drag himself up over the ledge, he balanced all his weight on his toes, he was startled to see that he was looking up into the eyes of a huge wedge tailed eagle.

The eagle was standing tall on top of the carcass of a wallaby. With a combined height of the eagle, on the wallaby and on the rocky ledge, from the perspective of Gellibrand dangling on the cliff edge, it looked the size of a man. It was only an arms-length away from Gellibrand and it did not move. The deep black eyes of the eagle looked deep into those of the Englishman, the light wind slightly ruffled the glossy bronze feathers that flared at its neck, but this was the only silent movement Gellibrand saw in those few moments, that seemed to go on forever.

As Gellibrand stared frozen into the eyes of the massive eagle standing above him, he became aware, only when it was too late, that he was teetering backwards on his toes and had no hold for his hands that dragged over the flat rock ledge. He scrambled desperately with fingers scratching feebly at the rock trying to find a crack or crevice, but he was already falling. He was calm then. He watched the eyes of the eagle watching him as he departed the ledge completely and accepted the open space around him. All he heard in his ears was the soft wind that accorded with the soft ruffle of the feathers on the thick mane of the majestic bird.

Murnin made a sharp involuntary squeal when she saw Gellibrand falling backwards from the top of the cliff above. The sound made Jacky stop climbing and he looked up just in time to press himself close to the cliff and watch the large lump of a body pass swiftly and silently by, before it landed with a heavy and sickening thud on the flat rock below. As

Jacky looked down, shocked by what had just happened, he saw the body of the man, flat on his back and the dark red blood that quickly formed a pool around his head. The lifeless eyes of Gellibrand stared up into the sky.

When Jacky reached the ground, Murnin was crouched beside Gellibrand, she looked at the man's face with a pitiful and sad expression. She held her fists to her chin like one who might be praying. Jacky crouched also and with both hands he rolled the limp body over. Laying him face down to expose the extent of the gruesome injury. Gellibrand's scalp has split open at the back revealing a caved in area of skull. Jacky looked at Murnin, and without the need for either to say a word, he took her hand and they hurried away almost silently across the log, over the river, and into the tall trees.

In a thick stand of bracken ferns a few hundred yards up the track, going uphill to the north, the boy sat up alert. He put his hand over the girls mouth to stop her giggling further while she laid naked on her back in the soft litter of forest floor. Sitting up the boy's eyes were just about at the same height as the level of the tops of the ferns. He scanned the bush carefully all around him. He was certain he heard someone passing. The girl went quiet and her expression turned serious when she realised the boy's concern.

As the boy scanned the area, with the expert eyes of a trained hunter, his attention turned to the sudden movement and squawk of a pair of black cockatoos that alighted from high up in a tall eucalypt about 20 yards further along the track to the north. Both he and the girl watched as the large birds circled gracefully around above them in the canopy of the forest and squawked loudly. Neither of them noticed the man and women slip passed so swiftly and light on their feet that it seemed they barely touched the ground as they ran along the bush path.

"The black cockatoos are heading back out to the open plains" the boy observed, as the birds gave another loud cry and flew away up the hill, "it's going to be a good couple of days," he laughed out loud, as he dropped again onto his back beside the giggling girl.

Bibliography

Newspapers
Colonial Times (Hobart)
Hobart Town Gazette
Sydney Gazette
Sydney Monitor
The Cornwall Chronicle (Launceston)
The Sydney Herald
Van Dieman's Land Advertiser

Books
Critchett, J. *A distant field of Murder*, Melbourne,
Melbourne University Press, 1990
Cunneen, C, and Libesman, T, *Indigenous People and the
Law in Australia,* Melbourne, Butterworths, 1995
Ellander, I. and Christiansen, P. *People of the Merri Merri,*
Melbourne, Merri Creek Management Committee, 2001
Kenny, R, *The lamb enters the dreaming. Nathanael Pepper
& the ruptured world,* Melbourne, Scribe, 2007
Gibin, R.W. *The early history of Tasmania*, London,
Methuen & Co. 1928.
Le Griffon, H. *Campfires at the cross,* Melbourne, Arcadian,
2006

Moorehead, A. *The fatal impact,* London, The Reprint Society, 1967.

Morgan, J. *The life and adventures of William Buckley,* Hobart, Archibald Macdougall, 1852. Reprinted in Sydney by McPherson's, 1996.

Mulvaney, D.J. *The prehistory of Australia,* London, Thames and Hudson, 1969

Stone, Carolyn. R. *Old Hobart Town and environs*, 1802-1855, Lilydale, Pioneer Design Studio, 1978.

Websites

Settlement of the Geelong District, compiled by Russell Hudson, www.freepages.rootsweb.com/~russellhudson/genealogy/hd-geelong.htm, accessed 31/12/14.

Australiaforme, www.honeycombe archive.com/thegreatwork/07books/books/AFM/book88.h ml. accessed 23/10/17

Letters from Victorian Pioneers, https://trove.nla.gov.au/work/9552249, accessed 09/11/17

Lara Heritage Review Phase 2: Draft Thematic History, February 2013, https://www.parliament.vic.gov.au/file_uploads/_1.2__14-11-20_Lara_Heritage_Review_Volume_2__February_2013__k8P6qtP4.pdf accessed 23/10/17

Eastern Portion of Australia (map), https://nla.gov.au/nla.obj-231341422/view accessed 10/05/16

General
State Library of Tasmania
(including Letter, Joseph Tice Gellibrand, to H. E. the
Lieutenant Governor, dated 30th August 1836, Hobart
Town.)

www.ingramcontent.com/pod-product-compliance
Lightning Source LLC
Chambersburg PA
CBHW020143120726

47903CB00007B/2385